# A TEMPORARY AFFAIR

Cass Bryson is persuaded by her twin sister Lila to attend a celebrity party in her stead, accompanying the enigmatic photographer Finn Mallory. Then, when his secretary falls ill, he asks Cass to take over her job temporarily. Though she can't deny her attraction to her new boss, Cass is lacking in self-confidence, not least because of the scars she bears from a tragic accident. But Finn is drawn to Cass too, and it seems they might just find love together — until Lila returns, determined to capture his heart for herself . . .

*Books by Carol MacLean*
*in the Linford Romance Library:*

WILD FOR LOVE
RESCUE MY HEART
RETURN TO BARRADALE
THE JUBILEE LETTER
FROZEN HEART
JUNGLE FEVER
TO LOVE AGAIN

CAROL MacLEAN

# A TEMPORARY AFFAIR

*Complete and Unabridged*

LINFORD
*Leicester*

First published in Great Britain in 2016

First Linford Edition
published 2016

A catalogue record for this book is available
from the British Library.

ISBN 978–1–4448–2731–6

Published by
F. A. Thorpe (Publishing)
Anstey, Leicestershire

Set by Words & Graphics Ltd.
Anstey, Leicestershire
Printed and bound in Great Britain by
T. J. International Ltd., Padstow, Cornwall

This book is printed on acid-free paper

# 1

'You want me to do *what*?' Cassandra Bryson's voice rose to a little squawk at the end, earning her hostile glares from her co-workers nearby. She turned away and whispered into the mobile phone, 'Are you crazy? I can't just walk out of my job and fly to France.'

'You don't even like your job. Besides, you can be back by tomorrow. Please, Cass . . . for me.' Lila's voice took on a sweet, pleading tone. One that had worked successfully before on her twin sister.

Cass felt herself begin to give in. Lila was right. She did hate her job. She worked in the typing pool of a small office, taking dictation and producing endless dull letters and memos for impatient staff. It was so dead-end that she could give it up and find similar work easily the next week. So it wasn't

1

her job that was the problem here. It was what Lila was asking — no, *demanding* — that she do for her.

'Tell me again why exactly you feel you have to follow this guy across the continent for a party?'

'Because Finn Mallory is not the kind of man you want to let down. This party is really important to him, and he asked me to go with him as his partner. Something's come up and I can't leave now, but you can. I guarantee he won't notice the difference, we look so alike; all you have to do is smile and hang on his every word for a few short hours.'

'Why does his name sound familiar?' Ignoring all the holes in Lila's theory of how the evening would go, Cass took her phone and walked out into the hall, trying to ignore the frowns and mutterings behind her. She closed the back office door and leaned against the wall. She wouldn't be missed if she did leave. It was her own fault for keeping to herself and not socialising with the

2

other women. They had asked her to join them a few times when she first started, but as she'd kept saying no, after a while they'd ignored her. She didn't mind; in fact, she was relieved when they stopped inviting her out. It was much easier to be left alone to get on with her tasks.

She tucked the phone between her cheek and shoulder to listen to Lila's reply while she tugged the sleeves of her long cotton blouse down over her wrists. An automatic gesture, so often done that she didn't even notice she was doing it.

'That's because you've probably read about him in the magazines. Finn's a renowned photographer. He specialises in photographing the hidden worlds behind everyday places. You must remember his exhibition on the back alleys of Rome?'

Cass didn't. And didn't care that she'd missed it either, or that Finn Mallory, whoever he was, was famous. She felt a familiar wash of tiredness lap over her. Lila and she might be twins and similar in looks, but they were very different in personality. Lila was as bubbly, energetic and lively as Cass was quiet, shy and retiring. Lila was the elder, being born a minute before Cass, and the result seemed to be a bossiness that Cass inevitably yielded to.

'How can you be so sure he won't know I'm not you?' she queried. 'How long have you known him for?'

'Not long,' Lila said, vaguely. 'I met him recently at a function and we got along well. He's a nice guy, just a friend, but I don't like to break a promise. This party in Biarritz is the promo launch of his new assignment, and I suppose he needs a beautiful woman on his arm. Thing is, even if he does realise you're not me, it won't matter as long as the paparazzi get their shots.'

This last was said with a laugh, but Cass could imagine Lila at the other end of the connection tossing back her long, white-blonde hair proudly. She

4

knew how gorgeous she was. Lila was the pretty one. Cass was the clever one. A childhood saying. It gave her a tiny slice of pain hearing the echo of her parents' proud boast about their little girls from so long ago. A prophecy that had come true. Lila was very pretty. And Cass was not. She shuddered and pulled her sleeves down again, glancing once, twice to make sure her arms were out of sight.

'So . . . can I count on you?' Lila asked.

There was a long pause in which Cass stared out of the window in front of her at the dull London summer. Around her were the sounds of clattering keyboards and phones ringing, the gabble of the office staff, the rustle and slide of folders and files, and the tinkle of the front office door as people came and went. Behind her, she could hear the grumbling of the girls in the typing pool, and one sudden raucous laugh with a tinge of maliciousness, so that she knew for certain they were talking about her.

'Where do I get the plane?'

\* \* \*

Cass shivered in the light breeze. The taxi had dropped her at the private airfield, and she was now standing on the tarmac with two suitcases and a hastily-scribbled set of instructions from Lila on how to get from the airstrip on the other side of the Channel in France to the party in the seaside city of Biarritz. Her surge of confidence as she walked out of her job had gone, to be replaced by uncertainty and a ripple of unease. This was not the sort of thing that she did. It was impulsive and risky. A sour taste caught her throat and she swallowed. Then she took a deep breath, grabbed the handles of the suitcases, and trotted as quickly as possible towards the pilot of the light aeroplane waiting on the runway. If she went fast, surely she'd be on the plane before she changed her mind. Under her breath, she cursed Lila.

'Hi, I'm Bob Rannigan, your pilot today,' the man said politely as she reached him.

He took her cases and stored them for her. Cass hesitated.

'Where is Mr Mallory? I thought he'd be here.'

Bob Rannigan looked embarrassed. 'He's already flown out, Miss Bryson. He was on a schedule and couldn't wait. But don't worry, the wind direction is in our favour today, so we'll be making up good time and won't be too far behind him.'

Cass glanced at her watch. Really? He'd gone without her. Or, rather, without Lila. How rude. She wasn't even an hour late. Once she'd made her decision, she'd gone as fast as possible back to her rented apartment to pack a small overnight case. Lila had promised she'd be back the next day, so there was no point in taking too much. Besides, she didn't have much in the way of choice of clothes. She grabbed her one nice dress and matching shoes, night-wear and undies, a bag of basic cosmetics and shower stuff, and that was her done. Only to find that when she reached the airfield, there was another suitcase waiting for her. It was much larger than her overnighter and it was Lila's. The paper message stuck to the top of it had all the instructions Lila thought Cass would need — plus a note telling her to use Lila's clothes, as they had to be better than hers.

She could have been offended by that comment, except she knew it was true. Lila loved partying and was out almost every night of the week. She had the wardrobe to go with it.

So here she was, and she admitted feeling a sense of relief that Finn Mallory wasn't here. Okay, she was putting off the fact she had to meet him, but it gave her a few more hours to prepare, even if she wasn't sure for what. How would he react when he found out she wasn't Lila? He was bound to be angry that he'd got second-best instead. Still, if he and Lila were simply friends, then maybe it wasn't too bad. Anyway, it was only one evening out of her life, she reasoned, settling into the window seat and fastening her seat belt. She calculated she could be back in London by midday tomorrow if all went well.

'What's he like?' she couldn't help asking Bob as he went past her, checking all the storage was secured.

'Finn? He's a good boss,' Bob said, adding: 'He likes everything to be in order, shipshape — or, rather, plane-shape.' He grinned at his own joke.

Cass thought he sounded awful, like a control freak.

Bob signalled to her that they were about to taxi along the runway, then he put on his headset and she was left to her own devices. She looked about Finn's private plane. Obviously the man was extremely well-off, seeing as he owned at least two private aircraft. The interior of this one was all leather and dark, polished wood for the seats and tables. There was a lingering hint of a spicy scent, perhaps aftershave. Bob Rannigan hadn't smelt that way, so it had to be the mysterious Finn's. She sniffed. It was . . . enticing. Apart from the furniture, she realised there was nothing else except the necessary cockpit, bathroom and tiny area for preparing food and drinks. It was neat and tidy and soulless.

Cass made a face. There was nothing to tell her about her companion of the evening at all. Except that maybe he was one of those people that colour-code their books and CDs, and line up pencils. Great. Perhaps that was why Lila had weaselled out of going. She hadn't given Cass a reason for her inability to go. Said she'd tell her later. Cass could have sworn she heard a man's voice in the background just before she pressed 'disconnect' on her phone. She didn't put it past Lila to have found a new boyfriend she simply couldn't bear to part from, promises or no promises regarding French celebrity parties.

She sighed and leaned back in the comfortable chair. She'd find out soon enough what Finn Mallory was like. Since it was a short trip, did it really matter? If she hated him on sight she would be out of France by the next day. And she'd make sure Lila didn't ask for any more favours for quite a while.

&#42; &#42; &#42;

The hotel was the most fantastic candy-pink colour, like a dolls' house, with white curlicue window sills and curved shutters that plastered the walls as if they were made of icing sugar. The strong, bright sunlight made everything even sharper, and it hit Cass's shoulders with searing, welcome heat.

She stepped nervously inside and a concierge came forward to greet her. Soon she was standing in a spacious hotel room on the third storey, with her suitcases propped on the floor, staring out of the window at the intense blue waves of the Atlantic Ocean crashing onto mile after mile of golden sand. The beaches were covered in people sunbathing and swimming in the surf, and for a moment she longed to join them. It was over five years since she'd been to the seaside. But Cass turned away and pulled the drapes across the window. It wasn't possible for her.

She re-read Lila's instructions for what seemed like the millionth time. The party was going to be downstairs in the ballroom. She'd had a glimpse of it on the way up the stairs. A huge space with a polished wood dance floor, long, sinuous bar, and crystal chandeliers. Finn Mallory was to give a brief presentation and photo opportunity for the press, and then the party proper would begin.

Cass's jaw tightened; she deliberately lowered her shoulders and took several deep and steadying breaths. She was way out of her comfort zone. Lila had no right to ask her to do this. She balled her fists but let them go. It was no good getting angry at her sister. Lila was Lila. As selfish and charming as they came. And Cass loved her. She should instead be angry at her own body for the way it ratcheted up the tensions in her skin and bones in every situation.

For distraction, she opened the larger suitcase and spread out the clothes. What was suitable? There was a variety of dresses, skirts and tops to choose from. She picked out a dress in midnight blue which was velvety and gorgeous. When she shook it out she saw the bodice had silk straps and no sleeves. With a sigh of disappointment she laid it down. In the end she opted for a light turquoise dress, with matching delicate sandals on outrageously high heels. There was a silk evening wrap to go with the dress, and if she was careful and kept it around her, then it would be okay.

After her shower, she dried her hair and got dressed, then applied her makeup with careful precision. She studied her image in the full-length mirror. The dress suited her, because it suited Lila. Cass frowned. She took her hairbrush and smoothed down her long hair. She was ready. She pulled her wrap across her shoulders and arms and picked up her evening clasp bag.

Her heart was thudding in her chest as she took careful steps down the thickly-carpeted stairway. Below in the ballroom there was the noise of the party guests and the click and flash of cameras. She was a little late and the presentation had begun. Curiously, she paused on the stairs and gazed in to the ballroom. There was a podium set up near the entrance. A tall, broad-shouldered man in a dark dinner jacket stood at it, with his back to her. The press surrounded him and she caught his deep tones in the snatches of sound between the cameras and the shouted press questions. She noted that his hair was chestnut and a little too long, curling onto the collar of his crisp, white shirt. It had to be Finn Mallory.

Feeling glad that no-one had noticed her, Cass slid quietly into the ballroom and veered left away from the podium and the press scrum. She waited beside a small potted palm tree, wondering if she ought to get a drink, praying that no-one would come over to speak to her and wishing that the ground would melt away and take her with it.

Even as she thought that, a slender woman with brown curls came and stood beside her. Her mouth was open and and Cass waited for her to speak. Instead, the woman took a sharp breath in and winced.

'Are you alright?' Cass asked quickly, her nerves momentarily forgotten.

'I've been really stupid,' the woman groaned. 'I know I've got to take care of my back and what do I go and do earlier today? Pick up a box of disks and files. Which was far heavier than I realised. I think I've twinged something badly.'

The skin around her mouth was white.

'Can I help?' Cass said. 'Do you want me to help you upstairs or get you a doctor?'

The woman shook her head. 'That's very kind of you but I'll be okay, I guess. I'm sure it'll be better by tomorrow. It has to be. I'm Liz by the way.'

'Nice to meet you, I'm Cass. Is there going to be a problem for you if it isn't better by tomorrow?'

Liz flicked a glance over at the podium, where Finn Mallory was still speaking.

'Yeah, see, that's my boss.'

'Is he difficult to work for?' Cass asked. It looked like she was going to find out more about her companion of the evening before she met him. It couldn't do any harm, she decided.

'Difficult?' Liz laughed then rubbed her back ruefully. 'Tough and exacting. And that's on a good day.'

Her eyes followed Cass's curious gaze to the man at the centre of the crowd.

16

'Don't be fooled by his good looks,' she warned, sounding half-serious. 'The man may be charming and he has no shortage of female admirers and *affaires de coeur* but his heart is never involved. There are a lot of sadder, wiser women around because of Finn.'

She was warning the wrong person, Cass thought. She had no intention of engaging that side of Mr Mallory. She was simply here on Lila's behalf.

'Honey,' Liz said, 'I gotta go. No thanks to the offer of help, I can make it up to my room myself, and I don't want to spoil your evening. I'm gonna take some painkillers and get an early night. Enjoy the party.'

Cass watched her go. She had warmed to Liz immediately. She hoped she'd be okay. She made a mental note to ask at reception in the morning for Liz's hotel phone extension. She would phone and see how she was or if Cass could help her in any way.

There was a hush and dispersal of the crowds. The formal launch and presentation was finished and the guests sought the buffet and the bar. Panic took hold of her. What had she been thinking? Lila was wrong. She couldn't do this. Even to help out Lila's friend. She turned blindly towards the exit but her way was suddenly blocked by a tall man. She made out a blunt jaw, strong nose and ocean-blue eyes before her gaze dropped to the floor, ready to ease round him with apologies.

'Lila, you look fantastic as usual.'

And Finn Mallory leaned down and put his warm, firm lips onto hers with a demanding and hotly seeking kiss. Instinctively, her mouth opened under his and when their tongues met, Cass felt the dizziness of sweet desire lick right through her. Then shock swiftly followed. At the same moment, Finn drew back from her with a puzzled frown. He was about to say something when an older, well-dressed man called to him. Finn shot one more stare at her before his companion insisted on taking him away to a group of older women, all shiny jewellery, painted lips and expensive outfits.

Cass touched her mouth. Her lips still tingled under the pressure of her fingertips. She had *never* been kissed like that. Then, hot on the heels of that revelation, she thought, damn you Lila. Finn Mallory was no friend of her sister's. He was clearly Lila's lover.

# 2

Finn's head was reeling. It was Lila, and yet it wasn't Lila. That kiss. What was going on? Bill Hamilton had finished an anecdote and was laughing. Finn gave a polite laugh, to show he was listening. Bill, after all, was one of his most generous sponsors and he had to network and socialise this evening. He hated it but accepted it was part of the job. Bill's wife, Nancy, was asking him a question about his travels and Finn was able to answer almost automatically, having heard the same question before. They always asked the same questions. How did he survive in the Namib Desert? Wasn't he afraid in the ghettos of São Paulo? Was it true he'd broken his leg falling off a rope bridge in Nepal?

His gaze searched the room. There she was. A waiter was offering her a drink and she was talking to him. Finn took a moment to drink in her beauty. The combination of that long, straight white-gold hair and turquoise eyes was mesmerising. Combine that with her long legs and slender curves, then it wasn't surprising that every man in the room had flicked an interested glance towards her.

He murmured an excuse to the Hamiltons and escaped their circle. He eased through the throng of guests, his height giving him an advantage over most of the crowd as he zoned in on Lila. As he approached, he heard her speaking to the waiter in fluent French. Which was a surprise. Given that when he brought Lila to Paris for a weekend, she hadn't even managed so much as a 'bonjour', telling him self-deprecatingly that she was too dumb to learn another language.

Finn's curiosity and anger grew in equal measures. He was rattled. He was a man who liked, no *needed*, to have everything under control. He planned his days meticulously. His personal assistant was under strict instructions to iron out any wrinkles that appeared in his daily agenda. And the woman in front of him was most definitely a wrinkle of magnitude.

Her eyes widened as she saw him. The waiter had gone and she was standing alone by the door, gripping a champagne flute like a defensive weapon. She was not Lila. Her eyes were not turquoise after all. Instead they were a light sea-green like the enticing smooth water of a warm lagoon. He thought whimsically of mermaids. And she was thinner than Lila. He felt he could encircle her waist with one hand. Her cheek bones were accentuated and her skin was pale with none of Lila's high colour.

'Who the hell are you?' he whispered savagely.

She flinched. Finn felt a momentary flip of guilt. He'd spoken harsher than intended but he was more than annoyed. He'd been duped somehow, mermaid or not.

'Where's Lila?' he persisted, when she didn't speak.

He took her elbow firmly as if guiding her in a gentlemanly fashion but he didn't feel like a gentleman. She didn't resist as he marched them both outside onto one of the balconies which was thankfully empty. He closed the long windows behind them for privacy.

'Well?' he demanded.

A little pulse beat fast in the hollow of her throat but she answered him steadily in a low voice.

'You don't need to act like a bully, Mr Mallory. You've every right to be angry but I can explain.'

Her voice was like honey. It did things to his gut. Again it was Lila speaking, and yet it wasn't. Finn ran an exasperated hand through his hair, never minding that it left unruly peaks. He visibly controlled his anger. Whatever this was, he could sort it.

'Who are you?' he asked again.

She didn't give a direct response. She half turned away from him to look out into the dark velvet evening to the darker ocean and the buoyant, glittering stars. He caught a curl of scent, delicate like violets, from her hair. He thought of their kiss. The sweet delight of it that had left him wanting more. Hadn't he known right then that it wasn't Lila he was kissing? It was different. It was . . . He blocked it down. That wasn't fair of him.

'I told Lila it was a crazy idea,' she said finally, turning to him and capturing his attention with her large, luminous eyes.

'Where is she?' He was still annoyed but it was lidded and locked. Finn felt better. He was in charge of his emotions and this mess was going to be sorted out very soon. Once he knew who he was dealing with, he could shape the information and decide what to do with it. And with her.

'I don't know where Lila is. Probably dancing the night away at a London night club. I'm her sister. I'm Cassandra, or Cass.' Improbably, she extended a slim hand politely in greeting, as if they were meeting for the first time at the party and had never exchanged a passionate embrace that had left his pulse racing.

Finn stared in surprise and shook it. Her fingertips were cold against his wrist and her bones felt fragile as if he could crush them accidentally. He let her go and felt a strange reluctance to do so. Her touch trailed his palm before she hugged herself close under her evening wrap. It wasn't cold on the balcony. The opposite in fact. The night air was warm and sticky.

'Lila couldn't come tonight and she didn't want to let you down. So I came in her stead. She told me you were a friend. But that's a lie, isn't it Mr Mallory? From the way you kissed me, I'd say you were much more than simply friends.'

'Call me Finn,' he said, shaking his head in frustration.

A flicker of annoyance escaped the lid he'd put on it. She was able to talk so calmly about their kiss. Hadn't it affected her at all? It shouldn't bother him, but it did.

'Lila and I had a brief affair,' he told her. 'I was surprised when you turned up tonight. I didn't think she would. We had a weekend together a couple of weeks ago in Paris and I invited her to my launch here. I haven't seen her since.'

'That's rather odd, isn't it? Are you still together, or not?' She sounded genuinely puzzled.

Finn wondered just how naive she was. Did he have to spell it out? Her sister didn't give the impression of being a woman who liked a long-term relationship. They had given and taken pleasure in each other knowing that there were no deep emotions involved. It suited Finn. It was all he wanted in any of the women he dated. There was control in that too, he was self-aware enough to know. It avoided any complications. Nothing should come between him and his work.

Cass waited for his answer. She wasn't afraid of him now. He didn't realise how intimidating his height and broad shoulders could be. She had felt out of her depth as he stormed the two of them across the ballroom to the balcony. Had felt the rigid muscle in his arm as he held her elbow. She could've made a scene of course. Perhaps shrieked and tried to wriggle free. But his grip was like iron and she was not the sort of person to draw attention to herself.

Once they got to the quietness of the balcony she had calmed down. It wasn't as if he was going to bodily throw her off the balcony. So her courage had returned and she was able to answer him without fear. If only he wouldn't look at her as if he could see right through her. His gaze was uncomfortably intense. Those dark blue eyes seeking . . . something from her. He was downright gorgeous. The thought sprang up from nowhere. She should've known that. Lila only dated handsome men. But Finn Mallory wasn't exactly handsome. His jaw was too broad and his nose looked like it had been broken at some point in his past. Yet that didn't deflect from an overall impression of sexy, attractive *maleness*.

Hold on there, Cassandra. What on earth was she doing? Fancying a man that her sister might still be dating. She had to ignore the fact that he was at least a foot taller than any other man in the ballroom. That his hair was the colour of glossed chestnuts streaked with tiny glints of fire. That he was wearing the aftershave or scent that had lingered so temptingly in the aeroplane interior. A scent that was dangerously alluring. That, in fact, Finn Mallory was the most rugged male that she had ever met.

Cass pulled her wrap closer. It didn't matter anyway. Even if he wasn't in love with Lila, he wouldn't look twice at Cass. Not if he saw her for what she really was. Besides, she didn't need a man in her life, did she. She had managed so far without one. For five years. Before that, well that was another story, another lifetime. She bit her lip at the memories and looked up to find Finn watching her mouth. She ran her tongue nervously where she'd bitten the skin and his adam's apple moved as he swallowed. Suddenly the balcony was too small for both of them. A prickle of sweat formed on her brow.

'Well, now we both know where we stand, I'll leave you to your launch and go upstairs with my apologies once more,' she said briskly, hoping to break the strange atmosphere.

'Not so fast,' he caught her as she went.

He appeared to have come to some decision. She stared coolly at his hand until he removed it from hers. Really, he had a terrible habit of touching her. Which took her right back round to their kiss, where she didn't want to go.

'You owe me,' Finn said sternly.

'Since Lila isn't here to be my partner tonight, then you'll have to take her place. There are going to be magazine photos taken for the gossip pages tomorrow so let's go.'

Before she could protest, Cass found she was following his broad back into the midst of the party. It was hot and noisy and she was glad that he broke ground first through the bodies so she could lightly step after. He was right. She did owe him. It wasn't fair what she and Lila had cooked up for tonight. But it was too late to rewind. So she would stay and hang on his arm and hope the rest of the evening sped past. Cass was tired. She longed to go upstairs, pull off her party dress and slide into the comfort of her hotel bed.

'More champagne?' Finn asked and poured it into her glass before she could answer.

Cass took a sip. Maybe she should drink it. The more gulps, the more relaxed she felt. It was false confidence but it might just get her through the night.

Finn leaned in so close she felt his warm breath on her cheek. It smelt of wine and cherries for some reason. His lips were so close. All she had to do was turn just a tiny bit and their mouths would touch. It was like an itch she shouldn't scratch.

'We're more than friends, remember. You're my date for the evening, so let's act the part.'

He was punishing her. Punishing Lila. There was an edge of anger that simmered around him. Cass didn't blame him. But she didn't have to like it either. He moved decisively into the crowd, pulling her with him. He was in charge, his body language said loud and clear. She got the strong impression that was where Finn like to be. Firmly in command. It reminded her of how the aeroplane interior looked and her first impression of him as a control freak. Nothing he'd done so far had changed her opinion. He might be blessed with rugged good looks but his personality was far less attractive, she decided. No, she didn't like Finn Mallory one little bit.

But she had to admire his charm offensive. He moved through the ballroom, taking Cass with him, talking to everyone and answering questions patiently and with apparent interest. Cass took another glass of champagne from a passing waiter and sipped it like it was lemonade. Her head was pleasantly fuzzy and for once her body felt fluid and at peace. She liked the sensation. Not only that, she found she could converse quite easily with people she didn't know, although afterwards she had no idea what she'd said.

'What exactly do you do for a living?' she asked him, when for a moment they were alone together before the next onslaught of networking.

'You really don't know?' He sounded faintly amused. 'That's refreshing. I'm a photographer who happens to be rather well-known and for some reason I sell pictures as easily as candy.'

'What was all that about broken legs and bridges?'

'Ah, it's a long story. I'll tell it to you tomorrow over breakfast.'

Cass gulped at the insinuation in his remark. He didn't expect her to take Lila's role all the way through, did he? She glanced at him but he grinned innocently. She let a breath out. He was teasing her. That was all. She wondered where his room was, compared to hers and hoped it was far away. They might meet at breakfast but she planned there and then to avoid him.

At least he wasn't angry at her any longer. Now he was back in charge as Commander Finn, he was handling the evening very well. He looked to be having fun. Cass realised she was having fun too, sort of. Now the champagne had kicked in, the evening had taken on a softly surreal edge. She could see why Lila liked parties.

'Let's get some food,' Finn said suddenly, staring at her with concern.

Cass jabbed a cheeky finger at his chest. 'Not until you tell me about your latest project. What are you launching?'

'Have a canapé while I tell you,' he suggested, piling a plate of snacks and forcing her to take it. 'You look like you need to eat rather than drink right now.'

'That's rather rude of you,' Cass snickered. She swayed slightly but righted herself. Maybe she should have a nibble of spring roll. 'Come on then. Tell me what you're going to be photographing.'

'You've probably heard of my series 'Hidden Places'?' Finn said.

'Nope.' Cass shook her head.

He laughed out loud and it was a deep, growly sound that made her want to join in.

'You're not doing my ego any good,' he said. 'Don't you get out at all to exhibitions? Or watch television occasionally? Read a newspaper or two?'

'There's no need to be sarcastic. Not everyone likes to read about self-absorbed artists and famous people.'

'You'd have to be a virtual recluse not to have heard of me.'

He had hit the nail on the head, Cass thought ruefully. She didn't go out if she could help it. She didn't watch television or read the news much. But he didn't need to know why.

'Okay, let's cut to the chase,' she said bitingly. 'Let's pretend I have heard of you. So please, do go on and tell me what your French project is all about.'

He raised an eyebrow at her bitterness but shrugged and told her.

'Biarritz and the area around the Spanish border, up into the Pyrenees are very familiar holiday destinations. I don't photograph them. They've been filmed a million times over. What I do is seek out the unusual, the flip side, the undiscovered side of these everyday places.'

'And you're good at it?'

'Yes, I am good at it. That's not me being boastful, that's just the truth.'

She made a face at him and Finn was

wryly amused. He was right. She did nothing for his ego. She hadn't heard of him and she wasn't impressed. She was quite different from her sister. He knew that was why Lila had seduced him. Okay, she hadn't had to work hard to hook him in. He was attracted to her the second he saw her at the dull function somewhere in central London. Which red-blooded male wouldn't be? In a room of beautiful women, her looks were something special. Natural white-blonde hair, and skin that needed no makeup, it was so clear and fine.

He had no illusions though. Lila was more impressed by who he was, and by how rich he was. She hadn't bothered to discover the real Finn. He didn't want to show her. Mutual pleasure and no pretence. It had been a good weekend and he hadn't expected to see her again. Cass's appearance tonight had blown him away.

'You speak good French.' He changed the subject.

'You overheard me speaking to the

waiter. That's how you knew I wasn't Lila.'

Finn was impressed. She was quick. Against his better judgement he was intrigued by her.

'I'm the clever one and Lila's the pretty one.' Cass's words slurred slightly and Finn saw her glass was empty.

He took it from her. How much had she drunk? She swayed towards him and her head landed on his chest. Her hair tickled his chin. It felt soft and silky. He had the oddest brief sensation of tenderness before he steadied her away from him. Her green eyes glazed.

'Time for bed, Cassandra,' he muttered.

She shot him a panicked look and he realised he'd worded it badly. Then it conjured up images that heated his body. He damped them down.

'Your own bed,' he clarified swiftly.

He supported her across the room, making it look as if they were a couple laced together, arms linked and her head gently resting on his shoulder. Then they went slowly up the stairs. She gave him her key from her ridiculously tiny evening purse and he opened up her hotel room and she stumbled in and lay down on the bed.

'Where do you want me to leave your keys?' Finn asked but there was no answer.

Cass was asleep, her breathing deep and even and her chest rising and falling. Her evening wrap had slipped from her arms and lay pooled around her on the bed. Finn looked at her. Her upper arms were covered in pink, shiny puckered scars.

# 3

Cass groaned and sat up in bed. Sunlight streamed in a beam through a gap in the drapes, hitting her face and making her wince. Her head drummed painfully as if an army was marching on it. Her hair was a tangled mess and when she rubbed her face a smear of mascara painted her fingers. Great. She felt awful. It served her right for letting Finn Mallory boss her into staying at the party last night.

Finn. Snatches of their conversation drifted back into her mind. Cass cringed. She'd called him a self-absorbed artist. Worse, she now remembered sinking her heavy head onto his chest. Even worse, that broad expanse of muscle had felt good. No, not good. Fantastic. Like coming home. A safe harbour. She felt like a fool. Now she'd have to apologise for her behaviour.

Cass groaned again. What had she been thinking? The problem was, she hadn't been. The champagne had taken over her senses. It was all his fault. If he hadn't kissed her . . . She had to forget that. It was a mistake. He and Lila had a fling. He wasn't to know she wasn't her sister. Bluntly, she reminded herself that she hadn't kissed anyone in five years. Of course that kiss was going to be amazing. It was simply the monsoon after the desert, wasn't it. Besides, she could forget it now. There weren't going to be any more kisses. This afternoon she'd be safely home in London and she need never see Finn again. Lila owed her big time.

She gingerly swung her legs out of bed. Which was when she realised that she had no recollection of going to bed last night. Which led right on to the fact that someone had covered her with the duvet. It had to be Finn. Cass screwed up her eyes. She remembered climbing the stairs. Her face heated as she recalled leaning onto him for balance.

He had opened her door and helped her inside. Then, nothing. She must've fallen asleep right away. It was too embarrassing for words. She prayed she hadn't snored or dribbled in front of him. *Please*.

But the worst of it was that her arms were bare. Sitting on the edge of the bed, her head aching, Cass saw she was wearing her evening dress but the wrap was gone. No, not gone. Folded neatly on the spare pillow. So he had seen her skin. He knew how disfigured she was. She wanted, for a moment, to crawl back under the covers and curl up like a pill bug. Away from the world. But then she forced her head high. It didn't matter what Finn thought about her. She didn't like him, right? And after this morning she never had to see him again. She'd get her flight home and start looking for another job.

She took a long, hot shower and dressed slowly. She guessed that Finn was the kind of man to get up early and have the first sitting of breakfast. She planned to arrive at the hotel dining room well after he had eaten and left. She hesitated over her makeup bag, then decided not to wear any. It wasn't as if she had to impress anyone. Especially her sister's ex-lover. Or current lover. She really needed to hear from Lila.

As if on cue, the telephone rang. She picked it up, half expecting it to be Finn demanding that she leave for the airfield immediately to keep to his schedule. But it was Lila.

'Hey.'

'Hey yourself,' Cass replied sourly.

'I'm guessing here that he guessed,' Lila said, not at all put out by Cass's obvious bad mood.

'Yes, he did guess and was none too happy at the deception.'

Lila gave a chuckle. 'That's Finn for you. He hates for stuff to happen to him that he hasn't planned a hundred times over. Total control freak.'

'Indeed,' Cass sighed. 'But you neglected to tell me that. Just as you forgot to tell me you dated him.'

'No, I told you that.' A pause at the other end of the line. 'Didn't I?'

One of Lila's tricks. To swear black and blue to something that just plain hadn't happened. It was like a magic trick, where a bird appeared when a scarf was expected. Misdirection.

'No, Lila, you didn't tell me that,' Cass said through gritted teeth. 'The question is, are you still dating him?'

'How did you . . . Did he? He did, didn't he. He kissed you. Or did he try something heavier on?'

'No,' Cass said quickly. 'It was a brief kiss, that's all.'

Except it hadn't been brief. His lips had lingered on hers and the kiss had been deep and satisfying. And she had to forget about it. What if he had tried to touch her, to take things further? She shivered with mixed emotions. Then she realised that Lila had once more distracted her from the main point.

'Is it over between you?' she asked.

'Why do you want to know? It

doesn't matter now. You're coming home today. Thanks, little sis, for covering for me. Oh, Mandy says you can come and work in the café till you get another job.'

Lila worked in her friend's café as the assistant manager. Privately, Cass thought she could do better but Lila seemed to love it. Besides, she had no qualifications other than her looks, as she laughingly said, so she was never going to get a high-flying career.

When Lila said that, Cass felt a twinge of what could have been. If Cass hadn't ditched her university studies. Now she too was stuck in jobs going nowhere. Worse, she didn't mind. They were places to hide.

'Got to rush,' Lila was saying, 'I'm on late shift but I'm not even dressed yet. See ya soon. Come and find me when you get back, yeah? The café's open late tonight.'

'Wait!' Cass held her breath, listening for the telltale click of the receiver going down.

But she was in luck. Lila had heard her.

'What?'

'You told me you needed to go to the party because you didn't want to let a friend down. But that's not it, is it? It's a long way to travel for a party.'

As she spoke, Cass finally figured it out.

'You're hedging your bets, aren't you? I bet you've got another 'friend' there in your bed with you right now but you're still not sure about Finn. About letting him go. Lila?'

'Keep your voice down,' Lila hissed.

'If you don't tell me the truth, I'm going to shout and sing down the phone so your boyfriend hears everything,' Cass threatened.

'Okay. Just . . . speak quietly, please Cass. I'm going to go into the kitchen. Ant's here in the bedroom sleeping.'

Cass let out a very exasperated sigh. Lila was *impossible*. She was keeping Finn dangling while dating Ant. Although Finn didn't know he was 'dangling', she admitted. He hadn't expected to see Lila again. What had he said last night? He was blown away to see her at the party. But that kind of implied he was glad to see her. Which led on to the fact that Finn might want to continue their affair.

'This is so typical of you,' she said, keeping her voice to a loud whisper. 'You're cheating on both of them.'

She could almost see Lila shrugging carelessly. Lila's motto was to live life to the full. She lived it as if it was her last day on earth. Cass knew why that was. The accident, five years ago, had changed them both. They had diverged in personality sharply since that awful night. Lila felt that having escaped death she had to eat up life at a pace. While Cass lived every day with the consequences of what had happened.

'It's really none of your business,' Lila told her and put the phone down.

Cass stared at it in shocked surprise. Then she pushed the telephone away.

Lila could be such a *cow*. She glanced up at the wall clock. There was nothing more to be done. The last breakfast sitting was almost finished. She had to go down now or miss it entirely.

She put on her cotton cardigan over her white tee, which was matched with a light blue skirt, and headed for breakfast. Going in to find a table, the first person she saw was Finn. He was hunched over a table next the window and he looked very displeased.

★   ★   ★

Finn hadn't slept well. He had woken up to snarled sheets where he had rolled restlessly in the night. He had dreamt of Lila. Dreams of her lithe, smooth body and long, soft hair entwined around him. But when her face turned to his, her eyes changed in colour from turquoise to the green of coral seas.

He'd woken, bad-tempered, short on sleep and annoyed with himself. That kiss. If he'd known she wasn't Lila, obviously it would never have happened. But it had. And the devil of it was, that kissing Cass had been different to any woman he'd ever kissed before. It was as if there was a connection between them that was more than simply physical. A deep magnetism. Breaking off the kiss was like separating the powerful magic that draws the magnets together.

Forget it. He had to concentrate on the photographic project. That was why he was here. He was good at focussing single-mindedly. It made him the great artist he was. Yet he couldn't help his mind drifting to Cass as he showered and dressed and went down to breakfast.

He felt more like himself once he'd eaten the requisite croissants and drunk a cafetiere of good French coffee. Back in control. His schedule on the breakfast table in front of him, ready for the items to be checked off once completed. Which was exactly the moment that his cell phone rang.

It was Liz, his personal assistant, who'd travelled with him from New York. She was booked into a room on the first floor and he had arranged to meet her at breakfast to go through the plan for the day. Instead, Liz sounded hoarse and miserable.

'Finn? I'm sorry but I feel absolutely terrible. You know I suffer from chronic back pain. Well, I've gone and done it in again. I can barely stand up and when I do, it's agony.'

'Barely stand up?' Finn said, disbelievingly. 'Are you sure? Isn't it more likely to be a muscle ache? I can get reception to send up some aspirin.'

This was a disaster. He couldn't function without Liz. She kept him sane and kept his life organised just the way he liked it.

'My back aches something awful and I've got pain so bad I can't get out of bed. So, no Finn, it's not a muscle ache,' Liz snapped down the phone, then groaned as if even that was too much effort. 'You're gonna to have to cope without me. I don't think I can even travel home like this.'

Finn swore under his breath so Liz wouldn't hear. He was sorry for her, really he was but he needed her. Liz being ill couldn't have come at a worse moment. It took all his self-restraint not to bellow out that she had to pull herself together, back pain or no back pain and come sort out his calls, his travel arrangements and all the other admin that was building up on his tablet.

'Right. Just rest and don't worry about work. I'll get reception to send up medicines and hot compresses and to phone for a physio. There's no need to travel home until you're feeling better. I'll extend your room booking.'

Great. Now he was doing Liz's job. His jaw tightened as his mind filled with the trivia that all needed doing. He could contain it, shape it, sort it. He was Finn Mallory after all. He ran a tight ship as Liz or Bob would tell anyone who asked. What no-one questioned was why he was like that. It was an admirable trait, being organised. But no-one could guess that Finn had spent his entire life trying to shape chaos into order.

*   *   *

He closed the leather cover on his tablet and decided he needed more coffee. Looking up to find a waitress, he saw Cass entering the dining room. His heart gave a little flip. She was wearing a skirt that hugged her shape, showing off a slender waist and long, shapely legs. Her legs were bare and her skin, though English pale, looked smooth and silky. He imagined running his palms down them. Or up.

Finn shifted uncomfortably in his seat. He shouldn't go there. He tried to think about work but Cass was still standing there and so he couldn't avoid her. She looked awkward, hesitating there at the entrance as though pondering whether to join him or take another table. He didn't blame her after last night. He'd been angry with Lila and with her for their trick. It was just the sort of deception he'd expect from Lila. At first, he'd been disappointed it wasn't her. Then, being with Cass all evening, the disappointment had gone. To be honest, he hadn't thought of Lila for the rest of the night.

Once Cass had drunk enough champagne to relax, she'd been an amusing companion. He'd enjoyed the evening with her, even if the smell of her delicate scent and the occasional feathery touch of her hair had heightened his senses, leaving him confused.

Watching her now, almost sidling into the breakfast area, reminded him of why he didn't want to get involved, despite her obvious attractions. He was good at compartmentalising his life. He enjoyed the company of women but was careful never to let relationships develop. Therefore his ideal choice of lover was a good-looking woman who was out for fun and who didn't want anything further than a short-lived love affair. In short, a woman like Lila Bryson.

Cass was wearing an incongruous white cardigan over her top. Around him in the dining area were couples all dressed for hot sunshine. It was already a good twenty-five celsius and due to get hotter as the day progressed. Biarritz averaged twenty-eight degrees on a July day and here she was looking dressed for a cold London morning. Which was why he needed to avoid her.

The scars he'd seen the night before were bad. He hated to imagine how much pain she had suffered to get them. Clearly she hadn't come to terms with whatever had occurred. Instead she hid them under layers of unseason-able clothing and walked into public dining areas as if she wanted to merge with the wallpaper. She was a wounded bird, however lovely she looked right now coming towards him, a polite smile pasted onto her lips. He had nothing to give to such neediness.

'May I sit with you?' Cass said, sliding into the seat beside him anyway.

'Recovered from last night?' he asked mildly, putting his work aside to make space for her.

She flushed right up to the roots of her hair. 'I believe I owe you an apology. I may have called you self-absorbed. It was uncalled for. I'm not usually so rude.'

'I've been called worse. Besides, you weren't at your best by then.'

She frowned at him. Finn felt glad. She didn't like that. Maybe there was some spirit hiding in her after all.

'I had to practically carry you upstairs. When I put you on your bed you fell asleep in an instant and snored like an engine.' Why did it feel good to needle her? To try to get a reaction out of her. Way better than her defensive camouflage.

'I did not snore!' Cass protested.

There was a pause in which she glanced at him with those large, expressive green eyes. 'Did I?' A hint of tentative embarrassment in the question.

'No, I made that up,' he admitted. 'But you did fall pretty much into a coma. Perhaps you shouldn't drink.'

'I don't usually. Last night, I needed some courage. I probably shouldn't have relied on alcohol for it.' She sounded genuinely regretful.

'Well, thank you anyway for being my escort. The party went well and Bill Hamilton was pleased with its success.' Why did he suddenly want to reassure her? He should be reminding her instead of what Lila had done. But he wanted to see that little rueful smile tug at her generous mouth again.

'Why does it matter what Bill Hamilton thinks?' The waitress had arrived and Cass tucked into a plate of croissants and jam with a healthy eagerness.

He poured fresh coffee for both of them. 'Bill's my sponsor. When I was starting out, he recognised my emerging talents and in those days he was a real sponsor in that he paid me advances on payments. Otherwise I'd never have been able to buy the expensive camera equipment I had to have to take the shots. Nowadays, I don't need his money but he helps on the promo side, has lots of business network connections world-wide. He's a good guy and a friend.'

She had a habit of tipping her head to one side as she listened. It was endearing, Finn thought. As if she really cared about what he was saying. There was a little fleck of pastry on her cheek and without thinking he leant forward and swept it off with his finger. Her skin was warm and a zap of awareness shot through his nerves. She stared at him. He wondered if she felt it too. For a minute, it was as if all he could see in the room was Cass's face and her gaze like deep pools he could drown in. Then she fumbled the tiny pot of jam and it splattered over the plate and onto her white cardigan.

'Blast,' she said, annoyed, and the strange moment had gone. She mopped the red stain with a paper napkin but it didn't go.

'Take it off and I'll get the hotel cleaning service to wash it,' Finn said.

Cass shook her head. 'No, it's fine. Really. I'll change after breakfast.'

Of course she wouldn't take it off. Finn knew he'd set her a challenge. And she'd failed. He had a sense of disappointment. His first impression was true. She was wounded by her scarring and not just physically.

'Do you always look this fierce?' Cass asked, a bite of sarcasm in her voice.

'I didn't know I was.'

'You looked mightily displeased when I first came in the door. I take it, it's not me? It's you.'

Was she mocking him? Finn raised an eyebrow. Just when he thought he had her nailed, she surprised him. There was a backbone to the woman after all.

Although she'd just reminded him of his problem.

'My PA has come down with a bad back, leaving me with a real issue.' Finn blew out a breath.

Liz's illness was unravelling all his plans. Or maybe they had already started derailing when Cass turned up last night instead of Lila. Whatever. He had a bad feeling about the project and it hadn't even begun.

'Poor Liz, she hasn't recovered then?'

Finn was surprised. 'You've met her?'

'Last night at the party. She was worried . . . ' Cass broke off suddenly.

'Worried?' Finn said in a dangerously gentle tone. He frowned at her and she ducked her head.

Then she surprised him again by raising her chin and looking at him straight on.

'Yes, she was worried how you would react if she was still unwell today. Clearly she had a reason. You don't appear to be taking it well.'

'I don't think you quite understand

the problem,' Finn replied coldly.

'Maybe I do,' she replied coolly, 'I understand that you need a PA at short notice. I could offer to do the job.'

'You?' He left the question in the air and she flushed prettily.

'I have done a number of PA jobs in the past, Mr Mallory. I have plenty of experience.'

'Okay, you can do it.' Finn made up his mind. It made perfect sense. Where else was he going to get an English speaker at short notice?

'Are you sure?' she said, seeming taken aback.

'Of course. You offered and I'm taking you up on it. I'll pay you a generous wage. The work isn't onerous. Hey, you might even enjoy it.'

'What if I already have a job?'

'That I doubt. You wouldn't have offered to work for me, if that was the case. Am I right?' Finn leaned back in his chair, almost enjoying the situation. If only he wasn't desperate.

Cass shrugged helplessly. 'As a matter

of fact, no I don't have a job right now. I've been working in an office, which has been rather underwhelming. I'm only offering to fill in until Liz gets back on her feet. I was assuming it was only a temporary sort of thing and I'd like to help Liz out but . . . '

Okay, now she was fixing her gaze on him. It did things to his stomach that had to stop. Finn didn't want to examine his motivations too closely. It made logical sense, he thought briskly. Liz was out of action. Cass was here. Why the hell not offer her the job.

'Great, that's it then.' Finn jumped to his feet and clapped his hands together to indicate the interview was over. 'I'll let Bob know we won't need the plane. I'll tell Liz I've sorted the problem and we'll meet in an hour to go over the itinerary for the day.'

He left her staring at him, open-mouthed, and sauntered out of the dining room, looking more relaxed than he actually was. Okay, he'd sorted the issue of his PA. All he had to do was remember that Cass Bryson was off-limits. She was now his employee and that's where it ended. She wasn't the sort of woman he wanted in any case.

# 4

Cass stomped into her hotel room and threw her cardigan on the bed. It was ruined. The berry stains weren't going to come out ever. But that wasn't why she was mad. She was mad with herself. Why, oh why had she offered to take Liz's place as his PA? What had she been thinking?

She was trying to do a good deed. To help Liz placate her tough and exacting boss. Instead, he had practically bulldozed her into taking it when she thought twice about working for him and had started to backpedal on her impulsive suggestion.

She kicked off her shoes. A sneaky little voice in her head reminded her she could have said no. He couldn't force her take the job. On the positive side, she'd have an income coming in which couldn't hurt. Also, it was only until Liz was better. And surely it couldn't be too hard doing whatever Finn's personal assistant did. Taking calls, typing . . . whatever.

On the negative side, she was going to have to work with Finn on a daily, possibly hourly basis. She still didn't like him. Commander Finn annoyed her beyond words. And physically, she hated what his nearness did to her. Why was it that the tiny hairs on her arms prickled when he was close? Why had a jolt of electricity shot through her insides when he touched her face at breakfast? It was his fault she'd dropped the jam. Really, he ought to pay for a new cardigan.

Things didn't improve much when she met him later in his suite to go over the itinerary. In addition to a spacious bedroom, he had the luxury of a living room complete with a massive television, two overstuffed armchairs and a polished coffee table.

Finn indicated the low table, where a stack of papers were laid out. Cass sank into one of the armchairs. She bit her lip nervously.

'Liz usually deals with all this paperwork. So, this will be your job now,' Finn said. 'It's simple enough. Mostly we're talking faxes with project requests, invoices and so on. I'll show you Liz's filing and books system.'

He leaned over her to explain the top sheet. Cass caught a wisp of his aftershave. The same spicy scent from before. His jaw was freshly shaven. It was square and strong. It suited his broken nose and dark blue eyes. There was nothing feminine about him. A shiver of pure desire ran through her. He was too close. She moved back and caught his frown.

'Did you hear me?' he asked.

No, she hadn't. Cass flushed. She'd been too busy examining his features to listen to what he was saying.

'Sorry,' she mumbled. 'Can you repeat it?'

Finn sighed and gave her a stare. 'Is it too much to ask for my new assistant to pay attention for five minutes? This is the system you will need to know inside out.'

'It would appear that you know it perfectly yourself. You don't need a PA. You could easily handle all this.' Cass waved a hand vaguely in the air above the coffee table.

'In fact,' she added with spirit, 'I wouldn't be surprised if you created the book keeping system and then taught it to Liz.'

He actually looked angry for a second before he straightened up.

'Look, it's okay. I've done basic book keeping and filing before. I think I can manage this.' She felt suddenly confident. Even without listening to him, a glance at the papers showed her she could handle it. He didn't need to know how many dull temping jobs Cass had held over the last five years. It looked as if finally they'd be put to good use.

'I can sense you think I'm micro-managing my affairs.' Finn glared at her.

To put it mildly, yes. But at the expression on his face, she didn't say it out loud. She sent a silent message of sympathy to Liz downstairs. How did she cope with a boss who breathed over her shoulder constantly?

'Maybe you should trust me,' she said airily. 'After all, what can go wrong?'

Finn made a sound that indicated a wealth of uncertainty. She smiled sweetly.

'Try me,' she said.

Finn raised an eyebrow. His glance flickered over her like a caress. Wrong choice of words. Her skin heated. Finn coughed and turned his attention to the tablet.

'Here, you take this. I've written Liz's passwords down for you. Familiarise yourself with it and be ready to go out on site after lunch.'

All at once, he was clipped and business-like making her wonder if she'd imagined his reaction to her innocent remark.

Cass couldn't deny her attraction to the man. Her body sang when he was in the same room. But she didn't have to act on it.

'You promised to tell me the story of your broken leg.' A change of subject to break the strange mood descending on her.

'Not much to tell,' he said, standing there rigid-backed as if he didn't want to be having the conversation. 'I was travelling in Nepal between hill villages when I had to cross a large river. There was a rope bridge but unfortunately it hadn't been well maintained. As I crossed, one of the wooden slats broke away and my leg went through.'

'You could have been killed,' Cass said, appalled.

'Not really. I was almost over the bridge and I was on solid ground. But getting back to a hospital is another story altogether.'

'And?' Cass prompted, fascinated.

'And we need to get going. We're behind schedule already today thanks to Liz's bad back. I'll meet you in the foyer in an hour.'

His tone brooked no argument. She got the strong impression he hadn't wanted to share his story but had been too polite not to answer her question. He walked away, his shoulders squared as if in irritation.

If she needed any proof that they had nothing in common, he had just provided it. He travelled widely and took risks. While Cass preferred to stay home and keep away from trouble.

★   ★   ★

But she wasn't at home now. She was way out of her comfort zone. Cass stared out at the beaches along Biarritz's Golden Mile. They seemed to stretch forever. The sands were dotted with hundreds, if not thousands of holiday-makers sunbathing and swimming. The waves crashed onto the sands and there were coloured flags posted in wide gaps along the strand.

'The flags are colour-coded for danger,' Finn explained, following her stare as he drove the beach road north. 'That beach there has green flags so the water's safe. But if they change the flags to orange or red then there's a problem. The surf can be incredibly wild along the coast. Luckily our destination is a friend's private beach where the bay is sheltered.'

Cass didn't care about the strength or otherwise of the surf. She just prayed she wasn't going to be asked to swim. She was wearing a thin, brightly coloured cotton top and sarong-style skirt for coolness. The searing heat of the day was, if anything, increasing. Her forehead was damp and her hair felt limp.

She flicked a glance at Finn as he drove. He didn't look as if the heat was affecting him. He looked cool, in both senses of the word, she thought with a wry twist of her mouth. A white tee and khaki cotton trousers perfectly accentuated his tanned arms and coppery hair.

'What am I going to be doing while you photograph the hidden beach?' she asked, holding her breath for his answer.

'You're going to be taking notes and numbering the shots. Also I like some short descriptive pieces for magazine articles. Liz writes great copy. Can you manage that?'

'Sure,' Cass said, with relief. She could easily do that while sitting in the shade, covered up.

'Great.' He looked over at her briefly before concentrating on the road again. 'Some people wouldn't be able to write too easily. There's a knack to magazine scripts.'

'I said I could do it. I studied languages at college.' It came out abrupt and challenging. For some reason it hurt that he doubted her ability.

'That explains your fluent French.'

'I speak Spanish and Russian too. Though not quite as well,' she admitted.

'Oh?' He sounded like he really wanted to know why.

'I . . . I gave up my college studies.' How much to tell him? She owed him a part explanation at any rate. 'You've seen my scars,' she went on flatly. 'I was . . . there was an accident five years ago. It changed a lot of things. My studies for one.'

He didn't say anything and Cass wondered if she should've told him. When she risked a glance, he was looking ahead at the road. She was glad he showed no prurient interest. She'd experienced enough of that with some people.

Finn nodded. 'Sounds tough.'

She was relieved when he didn't ask more.

Instead he swung the car expertly right onto a sandy track between windblown shrubs and they bumped down the track to come to a stop at the private beach. It was stunning. A strip of honey-coloured sand and aquamarine sea. Surely it was a hidden gem, begging to be photographed. So why was Finn frowning? He took out his cell phone and checked his messages.

'Damn, that's a text from Sylvia who owns the beach,' he said, his brows drawn. 'She's been delayed getting down here.'

'Do you need her here?'

'She was going to model for me. I do like to have people shots as well as landscapes,' Finn explained.

His eyes narrowed as he stared at Cass. She was already shaking her head. No way. Not in a million years. But Finn was nodding as much as she was mutely saying no.

'Just a few shots, Cass. I'll take them from a distance. You won't need to get into a swimsuit. I'm thinking lone woman walking along an exotic strand line.'

'You promise you won't take close-ups?'

'Mmm hmm.' He agreed with a vague mumble, already rummaging in his camera bag and laying out an assortment of different lenses and other paraphernalia.

Cass slipped her sandals off and planted her bare feet on the sand. It was wonderfully hot and it crunched under her steps as she wandered down to the water's edge. There was no-one on the beach, probably because it was private she reminded herself, belonging to the mysterious Sylvia. A little dagger twisted in her heart. Was Sylvia one of Finn's girlfriends? It really was none of her business. Cass threw a pebble into the gentle waves with more energy than necessary. Lila had clearly been a short-lived affair. Finn hadn't expected to see her again. What was to stop him having a longer-term lover? Yet, when Cass glanced over at the parked car and saw his tall frame headed towards her, camera bag slung over a broad shoulder and sunshine glinting on his copper head, she couldn't imagine him two-timing Lila. He looked too . . . solidly honest. Besides, she smiled, a man who insisted on such impeccable organisation wouldn't surely want the complication of two love affairs overlapping.

He put his gear down at his feet. Rubbed his jaw, deep in thought. She smelt his scent. Was suddenly aware of his height above her. Her heart did that somersault thing. She remembered in time that she didn't like him. He bossed her about. He micro-managed. He needed to loosen up, big time.

'I'm aware I'm asking you to do more than a normal PA does,' Finn said. 'But you signed up to the job.'

There was no sympathy into his voice. He didn't expect her to argue with him.

'It's a sunny day and I'm on a beautiful beach in France, I'm not complaining,' she shrugged, pretending a casualness while her heart thumped.

It wasn't just his nearness, though that would be enough, her adrenaline levels were set so high where Finn was concerned. It was also dread of the photo shot. This wasn't what she'd signed up to when she agreed to be his personal assistant. She wasn't sure she trusted him to stick to distance shots. Wasn't he going to want images of someone swimming in the turquoise sea?

'Okay, let's get started. How about you start walking slowly along to the rocky outcrop at the end of the bay? But slow, so I can get a range of shots.'

'I thought I was going to number them and write descriptions? I can hardly do that if I'm the model,' Cass hedged, her toes curling into the warm grains as if they could tether her to the spot.

Finn shook his head. 'Don't worry about that. We can do that later. This is more important.'

★   ★   ★

Finn watched the slender figure move along the beach, her hips swaying in an unconsciously sexy way and her long, almost white hair drifting in the warm sea breeze. A sharp tug of raw *want* hit his stomach. He couldn't help it. It took all his self-control not to run after her and swing her into him so he could repeat their kiss.

Instead, he focussed his lens, chose his shutter speed and aperture and took his own notes which was a novelty. He'd begun as a lone photographer without an assistant but it had been a while since he'd had to manage alone. He missed Liz and her cool competence. What had possessed him to ask Cass to fill in? He'd argued that she was an English speaker, which might be hard to find at short notice, but that wasn't it. The truth of it was that he didn't want her to leave. Which made absolutely no sense since he had neatly pigeon-holed her as needy and emotionally damaged and therefore completely off limits.

He blinked hard. Focus, focus, focus on the work at hand. Wasn't his ability to do just that that kept him sane? So do it now, he told himself sternly. He steadied his favourite camera and snapped the images. Cass was further away than he'd hoped so he began to follow slowly in her wake.

He got photos of her neat little soles sunk into the wetted sand on the strand line. When he caught her up, she was sitting on the sands beside the outcrop of tumbled boulders and verdant shrubs that separated Sylvia's bay from the public beach north of it. Her blonde head was lowered onto her folded arms, her knees brought up. It was a defensive posture. An odd tenderness stole over him. Her shoulders, covered by her cotton top, were rounded as she hugged her knees. Her forearms were reddening in the fierce sunlight. She was wilting from the heat. He felt responsible. With her pale colouring, he should've demanded she bring a hat, shades and sun cream.

Finn laid his camera carefully on a convenient flat stone. Cass positioned like that would make a great shot but he didn't think of it.

'Hey,' he called softly and stood near her but not so close that he was in her space.

Cass looked up. There was a vulnerability to her that got to him, whether she meant to project it or not.

Finn reached for her. She looked surprised but let him bring her to her feet. Without speaking, he walked steadily backwards, taking her with him, into the lapping sea. Cass's gaze was caught on his and he couldn't look away. The water eased up over his legs and waist until they were both floating in the warm swell. It felt both strong yet gentle and there was no danger in it.

Cass let out a long, slow sigh and shut her eyes. Gently, Finn turned her so that he was cradling her floating body. Her hair covered them both like pale strands of seaweed. He looked down on the smooth, unblemished skin of her face, so close he could see the delicate lilac tracery of her eyelids. Her lips were curved and full and kissable. Finn tried not to see how the water had moulded her cotton top to her breasts, showing their rounded perfection.

'This feels wonderful,' she murmured, letting her fingers splay either side of her body in the clear water.

'You looked like you were gonna die on me from heat exhaustion,' Finn said, his tone deliberately light. He was back to thinking about mermaids.

'I don't have to even worry about sinking.' Cass's eyes opened and fixed on him from his upside down view of her.

'Yeah,' he said, 'this is an old relaxation technique I was taught years ago. Only it was in a swimming pool, not the sea.'

'You? You learnt relaxation?'

'You don't believe I know how to relax?' Finn said.

Cass slid out of his grasp, flipping over like an elegant sea creature to face him as she treaded water. He felt bereft now that she wasn't close.

'You're full of surprises,' she teased, splashing him ever so slightly so that he

79

might have thought it an accident. Until she did it again.

'I know I work too hard,' he admitted. 'That's why I took relaxation classes. I am self-aware enough to know that I have to work at not working.'

He splashed her back, lightly but with a little more volume. Cass yelped. Finn swam closer to her, concerned.

'Sorry, I didn't mean to . . . '

A great wave drenched him, spun by Cass's arm right at him. She was laughing, turning like the mermaid she undoubtedly was and swimming fast away from him. Finn roared and gave chase. She was fast but he had the benefit of longer, more muscled legs and he caught her round her middle and lifted her up as she shrieked. He had intended to throw her high into the water but her warm body was suddenly stirring up more than fun and he couldn't let go. Their faces were but millimetres apart and her mouth was open in laughter, the water drops streaming down her face. He wanted to lick them off. Her legs brushed against his underwater and his body hardened.

He pushed her away before she could feel the physical effect she was having on him. He swam strongly to the shore and pushed his way out to lie on the sands. Cass landed beside him and for a long moment they didn't say anything.

He opened his eyes to glance at her. She was pulling her sea-soaked top from her arms and he caught a glimpse of the scars before she saw him looking and covered them.

'Do you want to talk about it?' Finn said quietly. He lay back, gaze shut and tried to be as non-threatening as possible. He didn't know that he'd held his breath until Cass began to talk.

'Lila and I were back at our parents' home to celebrate our nineteenth birthday. I'd come from my university studies and Lila had taken a weekend leave from her job. It was going to be such a happy couple of days. We had our birthday dinner and opened our gifts. All four of us walked down to the pub in the village and then back late to home.' Cass's voice was flat and emotionless.

Finn found himself staying absolutely still as if any movement would stop her speaking.

'My Dad had a bad habit of smoking in bed. We'd told him a million times when we were growing up that it was a hazard but he'd only chuckle and ignore us; even Mum's warnings couldn't change him. I think he believed that nothing had happened all the years, so it never would. But that night, there was a fire. He must've fallen asleep with a lit cigarette. He and Mum didn't stand a chance. Lila got out miraculously unscathed but I caught fire.'

*Caught fire.* Two words that conjured up so much pain and suffering. Finn's whole heart went out to Cass in that moment. He wanted to scoop her up and shield her with his body. Instead, he sat and listened.

'I tried to save them,' Cass said, 'but

I couldn't get to their bedroom. There was too much smoke and heat and the flames were too intense.' Her voice was still flat but there was a tremor in it and her gaze was shiny with unshed tears.

'I am so sorry,' Finn said.

'It was five years ago.' She turned to him, 'I should be over it by now and in some ways I've come to terms with it. But the true horror of it never goes away.'

'I don't imagine anyone could get over such a terrible event,' Finn said honestly. 'But they say that time is a great healer.'

'It hasn't healed my skin,' Cass said with a humourless laugh.

Finn pressed her fingers. He couldn't seem to let them go. It felt natural, somehow, to hold her hand. She wasn't pulling away either. He hoped she felt some comfort from his touch.

'There's more to your story, isn't there?' Because he heard the bitterness under her laugh and he doubted it came from the accident itself. Cass had been heroic that night, even if she didn't appear to realise it. To go back into a burning house to rescue her parents had taken real guts.

'Yes, there's more but this part is sordid and predictable.'

'I want to hear it, if you want to tell me.'

Cass smiled but her eyes were sad. 'I was engaged to be married. To Tom. We were going to wait to get married until I graduated and he finished his post-grad research post. We had it all planned out, even to where we were going to live and when we'd have our first baby. After the accident, he was very supportive.'

But he'd left her, Finn guessed. The swine. He added a few more colourful descriptions to the unknown Tom. He wanted to punch the guy hard. If he had loved Cass, then how had he had the gall to desert her when she needed him most? But Cass was speaking again and Finn zoned out of his anger and back into what she was saying.

'Tom wanted to bring the wedding

forward. He wanted to look after me, to take away all my cares.'

'So what went wrong?' Finn was taken aback. The script wasn't going the way he'd guessed.

'One day, soon after I'd come out of hospital for yet another skin graft, we were in the bedroom getting ready for bed. I was getting undressed and I turned to say something to Tom. And there it was.'

'There *what* was?'

'I'd caught him unawares. The look of revulsion and pity as he saw my arms. It was gone in a flash but I saw it and I couldn't un-see it. You know?' Cass shook her head. 'I finished with him that night. He argued and blustered, he even cried but I knew I was right. He'd stayed with me out of duty. And if I'm going to be with someone, then I want them to be there for love.'

Finn saw the uplifted jaw, the pride and the hurt all there in the way she held herself. He had a sudden urge to kiss her and to take her cares from her.

He even leaned, just a little, towards her. She shrank, just a tiny fraction, back from him and Finn made himself relax back as if it hadn't occurred. He got it. The reason why she seemed to be hiding from the world. She didn't want any pity, didn't want to see people's reactions to her scarred skin. He couldn't even attempt to kiss her. Because, yeah, right now he was offering it out of sympathy. But wanting to give comfort surely wasn't a bad thing?

'Cass . . . ' he began.

He didn't get a chance to finish his thoughts. There was a holler from further down the beach. A figure was waving and coming towards them. Sylvia had arrived.

# 5

Sylvia had a summer house at the top of her private beach. She had opened the double wooden doors wide to the view and now Cass sat sheltered from the sun, writing up image descriptions at a table with a jug of ice-cold lemonade at her elbow. Sylvia was not Finn's girlfriend. Unless he liked them aged around seventy, plump and jolly with a head of grey curls. It turned out that Sylvia was Bill Hamilton's sister and another fan of Finn Mallory's photographic art.

'You must be poor Liz's replacement,' Sylvia said, on being introduced to Cass, and her eyes actually twinkled. 'Finn, what were you thinking? This girl looks completely frazzled from the sun. Come along Cassandra, and let's get my little summer shed opened up. You'll like it in there. You can watch me do my modelling stint for Finn while you try my homemade fizz.'

Cass glanced back at Finn as Sylvia guided her firmly up past the tide-line to a small building with multi-coloured roof tiles. Finn's face was serious, his camera in his grasp, away in the world of photography. He looked calm and in command. As if he had never listened patiently to her story of her life.

Cass had to admit, it was lovely to be out of the harsh heat. The summer house smelt of warmed resin and lemons. It reminded her of home. Her parents had had a summer house. Smaller than Sylvia's but with the same evocative smells of summer and sea-soned wood. She swallowed down a sharp pang of loss. Yet it wasn't loss alone. There was a mingling of happier memories too. She was getting better. Slowly. Weird that telling Finn had helped.

She had felt slightly sick when he asked if she wanted to talk about it. He had seen the scars. They weren't pretty in spite of all the operations. The surgeons had admitted they had done their best but they couldn't entirely smooth out the ridged, furled damaged tissue. Unless she went back for more grafts. Cass had said no. She'd had enough of hospitals and pain and recovery and unfounded hope.

She had waited for the look of disgust on Finn's face when he saw her arms. It hadn't come. His blue eyes hadn't changed. There was sympathy in his voice and the touch of his hand had come as a shock. Strangely, it had helped, his fingers on her palm as she spoke. That tingle of awareness ever present when she was with him but was overlaid then by a feeling of trust. Not a feeling she felt too often with other people.

She'd told him everything. Left nothing out. When she told it, it was always as if it had happened to someone else, not her. Like she kept a door closed over the raw emotions. She told the structure of her story but not the flesh.

Cass wondered what Finn had been about to say when Sylvia had arrived at the beach. Maybe it was for the best that she hadn't heard it. She could pretend that he didn't pity her like everyone else did. She could pretend to be like Lila. Beautiful, unscarred Lila. Who was surely the reason behind the unconscious, strong attraction between herself and Finn. They hadn't spoken about it but it was there like a three-dimensional shape, solid and hard to ignore. Yes, that was it. Finn had kissed her when he thought she was Lila. He wanted to kiss her again, she could tell. But it wasn't Cass he wanted so badly. It was her sister. A woman who had all the looks and none of the baggage.

That wasn't quite fair to Lila, Cass thought quickly. Lila had been affected too. But unlike Cass, Lila chose to blank out her guilt and chase butterflies instead. They had never discussed the night of the accident. Never dissected the events. Cass didn't blame Lila for running away. She was terrified too of the flames and the hell of the burning house. She had so nearly reached her parents' bedroom before being forced back. When she had screamed for Lila to help her there had been nothing. Lila wasn't there. Cass had stumbled, aflame, down the melting stairs to find Lila curled up outside foetally on the patio, crying and shivering.

Lila at least had a proper life to lead. She went at it full on and gave every impression of being happy. Cass had given up and hidden away. After the split with Tom, she had been, quite frankly, deeply depressed. Gradually it had been easier to take the easy route with life and take no risks at all.

A lazy bee hummed inside the summer house and Cass blew it away from her gently. So what was she doing in Biarritz working for the most gorgeous man she had ever met? The question bubbled up from nowhere. It stumped her. This wasn't risk free.

She put up a hand to shade her face and squinted into the sun. There they were. Down at the sea's frothy fringe. Sylvia was hunkered down and it looked as if she was collecting shells. Finn was kneeling, a bit away from her, taking shots with his camera from all sorts of angles. He gave an impression of serious single-mindedness. Nothing was getting in the way of his photography. It was implicit in the rigid muscle of his stance. In the way he gestured to Sylvia so that she moved, making her face visible to the camera lens. Finn was an artist at work.

Commander Finn was back in place. Cass pulled a face, took a sip of lemonade. But she couldn't tear her gaze from him. It struck her that he had deviated from his schedule that afternoon to take her swimming. She had enjoyed it. Enjoyed the safe, floating experience in his arms. The fun of splashing him. The sexy touch of his legs underwater when they accidentally bumped against each other. The liquid burn that flooded her insides and made her want to wrap her legs around him.

She could deal with the physical attraction to him. Just. But not the other. Cass had lied. She didn't dislike Finn Mallory. She was beginning to like him a little too much.

'She's quite lovely,' Sylvia said, pretending to collect another shell as the camera shutter clicked into place. 'Just your sort of girl.'

'Sylvia,' Finn warned, taking another rapid set of shots.

'Her aura though, is another story. I see muddy, forest green for low self-esteem. She blames herself for something.'

'Quit with the mumbo-jumbo,' Finn said, and rolled his eyes at Sylvia's satisfied smile. It was a conversation they'd had many times.

'On the other hand, with you, my love, I'm seeing pink-red and bright lemon yellow.'

'And that means?'

'I don't think I need to spell it out,' Sylvia laughed.

'Please do,' Finn said sarcastically.

She would anyway. He had been friends with Sylvia for too long not to know her inside out.

'Bright lemon yellow means a fear of losing control. We all know you like to be the boss of your own actions.'

He couldn't disagree with that. He knew he needed that organisational drive, that control to stay sane.

'So, the question is ... ' Sylvia drawled, elongating the moment and dropping the pretty, shiny shells one by one onto the sand, 'why do you feel like you're losing control?'

'Perhaps because you've messed up my 'sunshine and shells' collection I was planning in my head?' Finn sighed, and lowered the camera. There was no stopping Sylvia when she got like this.

'Or perhaps, because something, or should I say someone, is influencing you?' Sylvia asked innocently.

She turned deliberately to wave up

the beach to Cass, who waved back merrily.

'Which takes me right on to the pink-red part of your aura,' she added.

'You want me to ask what pink-red auras mean,' Finn said. 'But I'm not going to. I refuse to indulge in your new age, hippy . . . '

'Pink-red,' Sylvia said loudly, interrupting him, 'means new romance, passion and love.'

'Now you're being ridiculous,' Finn replied. He chose to ignore Sylvia's smirk.

Sylvia was wrong. He might feel an undeniable attraction to Cass but that had nothing to do with falling in love. She was simply one of the most beautiful women he'd ever met. Or rather Lila was. They both were. Clearly. They were twins. It didn't take a genius to work out that they were therefore both equally lovely. But that wasn't right either. They were different.

Finn suddenly realised it was over with Lila. When he thought he'd seen her at the party, he had been pleased and excited. Once he'd kissed Cass though, it had all changed. The kiss was different, more intense, connecting at a deeper level if he was honest. She had beguiled him all evening. She was nothing like her sister. Lila was shallow and selfish. She made no bones about it, which was refreshing. She knew she looked good and she wanted to feel good too. Finn had helped her there. They had had a passionate weekend but his heart had most definitely not been involved and neither had hers.

Cass was different. He would not tangle with her in a light weekend affair. She was not the sort of woman that would escape untouched. He sensed that. She felt things deeply. There were layers to her that he had yet to unwrap.

*Whoa! Hold it right there.* There would be no unwrapping. She was fragile and vulnerable. Therefore she was right out of bounds. Finn had no intention of getting involved with a woman who had so many obvious issues.

She had survived five years since her traumatic accident by camouflage. By melting into the background. There was nothing to say that she might not, even now, get flaky just like his Mom had done.

Finn knew he couldn't cope with that. He had his own demons to deal with. There was no way he was taking on someone else's. Even someone as lovely as Cassandra Bryson.

He stood up and brushed the sand from his trousers.

'Thanks, Sylvia, I've got what I need.'

'Good. What about a drink? I'm parched. Shall we join Cassandra?'

Happily, Finn thought, looking up to the summer house where Cass had her head bent over the table, working hard at her papers. Crazy that he felt glad simply walking towards where she was. Mad to let her large, green eyes make his chest tighten. Foolish to breathe in her delicate flowery scent and imagine touching her.

'We're finished up,' he told her, sounding harsh and unfriendly in his desire to keep things cold and professional between them.

Her gaze widened in surprise. Then she gave him a stiff nod. Great. He'd offended her now. But maybe that was for the best, Finn told himself. That way they knew where they stood with one another. He was currently her boss. She was his employee. Nice and simple. He would deal with his attraction to her by ignoring it. After a while, it would go away. He had been wrong to take her out swimming in the ocean. Far too intimate. He should've been working to his schedule, keeping to his own rules. Life was to be shaped and formed by his work. He was doing her a favour because there was no future for either of them in pursuing a flirtation.

The way she was looking at him now, Finn wasn't so sure he'd been in line for her favours anyhow. Cass's expression was frozenly polite as she gathered up the notebooks, pens and her purse. It was hard to believe she had lain in his embrace earlier in the warm sea and splashed him mischievously.

'Do you want to go then?' she asked briskly. 'Or are we going on to any other locations today?'

'As I said, we're finished. We'll go back to the hotel. I've got some calls to make and I'll need you to send some email responses.' He kept his voice brisk too and tried to ignore the pink flush on her cheeks as she nodded and kept her head down.

Sylvia breezed in, puffing from her walk up the beach and happily oblivious to any atmosphere.

'Lemonade? I could drink the whole jug. Finn? Cassandra?'

She poured out three large glasses and they stood in the summer house and drank the cool liquid with Cass and Finn both silent and Sylvia chirping in between sips. Finn was grateful when he finished his drink in record time and set it down firmly on the wooden table.

'Thanks again,' he said to Sylvia, 'Cass and I have to go but I'll be in touch once I've chosen the images so you can see them.'

He didn't wait to see if Cass had followed him out, but set off fast for the car. It feels like I'm running away from something, but I'm not, he told himself. This is for the best. I need to get this project under my belt and done and dusted and I do not need any complications. I don't do 'relationships'. Remember?

\* \* \*

Cass was forced to hurry after his retreating back. She had managed to say goodbye to Sylvia, who surprised her with a kindly but serious look.

'Finn is a good man,' Sylvia said slowly. 'He's been through a lot to get where he is today. But take my advice, don't get too fond of him. I saw the way you looked at him. I'm afraid it will only end in heartbreak if you let yourself get involved.'

Unfortunately she didn't have time to ask Sylvia exactly what she meant by that, as Finn was nearly at the car by then. But Sylvia's warning reminded her of what Liz had said about her employer. She looked ahead to where Finn leaned impatiently on the car waiting for her.

She was tempted not to hurry but common sense prevailed. She was employed as his personal assistant and therefore she was meant to help him, not hinder him. Still, it would have been satisfying to walk slowly to the car to let him see she didn't appreciate his manner, Cass thought. What had got into him? He'd practically barked at her when he got back from the beach. It was a contrast to the relaxed, fun guy she'd splashed in the sea.

Who was the real Finn? It was as if he had two completely different sides. Mostly he gave the impression of a workaholic, tightly in control of everything around him. But every so often, a different Finn Mallory sneaked out. She wished she could see more of the relaxed Finn. No. That was wrong, she chided. She had no wish to get to know him better. There was no point. They were so different. Even if they were attracted physically and they both knew it, it couldn't come to anything. Besides, Cass wasn't ready for a relationship. She was pretty sure she never would be. After her experience with Tom, she never wanted to be in that position again.

And Finn clearly was the sort of man that didn't want a partner either. He and Lila had had a short weekend affair. That was revealing behaviour. He obviously liked short, sharp love affairs which didn't get in the way of his work.

'Are you scowling?' she asked, as she slipped in to the passenger seat after he'd flung the car door open for her.

'What? No. Of course not.'

'Okay. Just checking.' Why did she want to tease him, to needle him when he was like this? Was it to bring back the other, nicer Finn?

She stretched out her legs and smoothed her skirt down. Then wished she hadn't as he glanced at them and turned deliberately to the windscreen. The car coughed to life.

'I'm just aware that we're over schedule,' Finn said shortly. 'There are calls I have to make to the States.'

Cass looked at her watch. 'They're five or six hours behind us, aren't they? So the later you call, the better surely.'

'I'll rely on you to make sure I make the calls at the right time,' he replied. 'That's what I'm paying you for.'

'Are you regretting giving me the job?' she retorted.

'Don't be ridiculous,' he said coldly. 'You haven't been in the position long enough for me to judge you on it. I'm simply reminding you that I am on a tight schedule. Liz never forgets it, that's why she is such a good PA. I'm sure you will soon get up to speed on what I like.'

Okay, so the nicer Finn wasn't

coming back. She was travelling with Commander Finn. There was a veiled warning in his words. If she didn't get up to scratch and quick, no doubt Finn would be only too glad to tell her so.

★   ★   ★

Cass's neck felt hot from the sun when they entered the hotel lobby. It was blessedly cool inside. She decided to go and lie down for half an hour if Finn was able to manage without her. Once he'd made his urgent calls she could take dictation for his emails and then she'd finish off her magazine notes. She had enjoyed putting the words down on paper in Sylvia's wonderful little house. Describing the sand and the heat and the smells of summer and trying to match her words to the photographs that she'd seen Finn taking. It was satisfying work, unlike any jobs she'd had previously.

She was going to ask Finn if he minded her taking a half hour rest, when she saw Bill Hamilton rushing towards him. There was a quick, serious conversation between the two men. Then she saw Finn scanning the lobby. His eyes lit on her and he strode towards her.

'There's been a break-in at my home in New York,' he said. His mouth was a grim line. He ran his hand haphazardly through his thick hair. 'My photographs, all my belongings have been ransacked according to my neighbour. Bill's been trying to reach me to let me know but my cell hadn't picked up at the beach. We need to get over there fast. How quickly can you pack?'

Cass was stunned. 'Me? I can't go to New York.'

'Why not? You don't have any other place you need to be,' Finn said bluntly. 'You're working for me right now and there's no way Liz can travel while she's incapacitated.'

Cass felt dizzy. She couldn't go to America. She didn't travel, didn't leave home if she could help it. She was only in France because Lila had begged her and had twisted her arm as usual. Lila always got her own way with Cass because of the guilt Cass felt. Not that Lila realised that and she wasn't going to find that out ever. But New York? No way. It was too far to go. It was risky and she didn't do risk. If he tried to argue, she'd walk away from the job. She looked up to tell him she wasn't going and stopped dead. Finn's face was strained and his jaw was gritted. He wasn't going to beg but his blue eyes said it all. Cass saw the pleading in them, even if he didn't mean to show it. He needed her.

'Alright. Give me an hour to get freshened up and packed. I'll meet you at reception.' Her voice sounded normal and calm and she was glad of that. It didn't reflect the turmoil in her insides and her instinct to turn and flee. Yet there was a small part of her that was excited too. She didn't understand it. There was an edge of danger and uncertainty that was surprisingly thrill-ing. Or was it the fact that she was going to be spending a lot of hours with Finn on his home territory?

# 6

Early morning New York was much like any other large city, Cass was relieved to discover. They were standing on the doorstep of a big, old brownstone building while Finn searched for his house key. Despite the early hour, people streamed past on the sidewalk clutching large styrofoam cups of boutique coffee, laden with briefcases and oversized purses as they went to work.

They hadn't spoken much on the flight over. Finn had dropped into his seat and almost immediately closed his eyes which Cass took to mean that he wasn't in the mood for chit chat. Still, she had one or two things she wanted to ask. And talking to Finn would take her mind off her nerves at travelling to a new continent, yet further away from London.

'So when you told me that the burglar had ransacked your photographs,
did you mean that metaphorically?' she
asked.

He opened his eyes and rubbed them
tiredly.

'No, I meant it literally.' He yawned
and plumped up the pillow meaning-
fully under his head.

Cass ignored the body language.

'But surely you'd have your photographs all digitised onto a computer
database? Finn? Are you awake?'

He muttered something under his
breath which Cass pretended not to
hear. He sat up and shook his head.

'I do appear to be still awake. It's
difficult to sleep when someone's
yammering in your ear,' he said.

'Well?'

'I should've had all my photos
digitised but I haven't. There's a huge
backload from when I was younger and
using slides. I've been meaning to get
them all scanned in and numbered but
I never got around to it. They're

stacked up in my spare room.' Finn sighed heavily. 'Or they were. I have no idea what I'm gonna find when I get home.'

Cass hadn't bothered him further. Finn had slumped back in his chair and fallen asleep. It had taken her much longer to settle. She was heading into the unknown and her body was on a high alert that she couldn't calm down. Every fibre was hyper-sensitive. She could hear the steady thrum of the aeroplane's engines and the deep and even breaths as Finn slept. His jaw was shadowed with bristles; he needed a shave but Cass thought him even more gorgeous with that and his hair unruly. He hadn't wasted a moment in getting ready to fly home. He was momentarily rough and ready and she liked it. Liked him.

She forced her gaze away from him. Tried to dampen the curl of yearning in her stomach. Concentrated on thinking about what New York would be like and how long she was likely to stay there.

* * *

'Got it,' Finn said, waving the metal key at her. He hesitated before inserting into the door lock.

Cass knew he was wondering what on earth he was going to see inside. He'd told her that he'd asked that nothing be cleaned up before he arrived home. He didn't want some well meaning neighbour to accidentally clear away a photograph or document or put them where he couldn't immediately place them. So they were going into his home just the way the burglar had left it.

She heard Finn swear softly under his breath. Saw his shoulders go back with determination and couldn't help it, she moved round him to see. Cass gasped. It was bad. Worse than she had imagined. There was stuff strewn everywhere. Cushions had been ripped and thrown from the big easy chairs, there was furniture turned upside down and a vase lay shattered in the middle of the room.

Finn moved through what was clearly the living room and Cass followed. He went up a set of stairs and along a narrow corridor and pushed open a door. Boxes of slides lay scattered all over the small space. Many had spilled open and the white squares of slides lay like jigsaw pieces or large confetti in random heaps and splays.

Finn groaned and sank to his knees. Cass ran to kneel with him. Her arm hovered over his bent back. Should she touch him? Hadn't she sworn to keep things strictly professional between them? But this was different, she reasoned. She was offering him comfort and that was all. The man was suffering.

She couldn't help it. Cass put her arms around him and hugged him tight trying to impart sympathy and strength in equal measures.

'It's going to be okay,' she said. 'We'll get it all sorted. I'm not going anywhere until it's tidied and catalogued. We'll both do it, together.' She was murmuring as if to comfort a child. The tone was more important than the content of what she was saying. But Cass knew she meant it. She wouldn't leave him, wouldn't leave the task until it was all mended. Because she couldn't bear to see Finn brought so low. This was his treasure. His life's work.

He clutched her too. Even though he was much larger than her, he was inside her embrace as much as possible. His head rested briefly on her shoulder and she kissed his hair softly. He wouldn't feel it, so light a touch it was but she felt an immense tenderness right there and then for him.

He brought his face up to speak to her. Cass kissed his cheek as a friend might. Except that he moved as she did so and her kiss found the edge of his mouth. His hands reached up to cup her face and he stared at her. Cass's heart thumped. It wasn't like comforting a child any more. Finn was all man. He let his hands drop and she felt an

113

intense disappointment. Finn turned back to survey the room.

'I don't know where to start.' He sounded helpless.

'We'll start by picking up the individual slides and stacking them on the table,' Cass said briskly. 'It won't take long to get some order into this chaos. Okay . . . '

She picked up the first forlorn plastic square.

★   ★   ★

Finn caught her hand. He had to explain. Make her understand. This wasn't just boxes and film. This was . . . *him*. All this represented his entire adult life. All the days he'd spent photographing and dreaming and working and suppressing the rest of his miserable existence.

He had startled her by grabbing her hand. An emotion he couldn't entirely identify washed through him. Here was Cass, who had her own problems, who had freaked at the notion of coming to America with him, buoying him up. She was trying to make him feel better. She was putting her own fears on hold to give him sympathy and support. He still felt the whisper-light touch of her lips on his hair. Her kiss so near to his mouth had almost made him lose it. It would be so easy to let go in Cass's arms. She didn't understand. But he suddenly wanted her to.

'This was my safe harbour,' he said slowly, taking the slide from her and rolling it edge to edge in his fingers. 'I know you think I like to be in control of things and you're right. I have worked long and hard at that control. The reason is that an ordered environment is the opposite of chaos. I was brought up in chaos and I swore when I grew up that I was never going back to it.'

Cass slid down to sit on the floor, legs to one side, reminding him of the Little Mermaid in the harbour in Denmark where he'd gone to photograph her. She was listening to him, her head tilted and her eyes never leaving his. It gave him the strength to go on with his story.

'My mother was quite a famous actress when she was young. She was the beautiful Margaret Conway who enlivened any film she was in. I can almost recall Mom in those days if I try hard. Of course I was a small boy then. Our lives changed when another actress threw acid in her face. They had been fighting over the same man and he'd chosen my mother over this other girl. There were hospital stays and surgery but Mom was never the same again. She became depressed and started to drink heavily. Soon I was bringing up my younger brothers and trying to keep house while being a child myself.'

Finn stopped. He wasn't telling it well. Maybe he should stop. He didn't want her sympathy, wasn't trying for it. He wanted to tell the tale without emotion, logically, so she could see why his image collection was important. So why was she staring at him as if she was going to cry?

'I'm so sorry,' Cass said. 'Where was your Dad in all this?'

Finn gave a harsh laugh. 'I didn't have a Dad. I have no idea who fathered me. Hey, I didn't need a Pop when I had so many Uncles.'

'Oh Finn,' Cass said.

He rushed on, not wanting to hear that trembling in her voice. This was why he never told anyone about his childhood and upbringing.

'That wasn't the worst of it. Mom never recovered from losing her looks. They were all she had, or so she kept telling us. They had been her livelihood. She forgot she had kids to care for who might have made life worth living. A few years after the acid attack, she killed herself.'

Cass's breath caught so sharply he heard it loud in the quiet room.

'It didn't end badly,' Finn said. 'We were brought up by my Aunt after Mom died and then we had the rest of a happy childhood and a family who loved us. But I swore then, that I was never going to live in the chaotic disorder that was the stamp of my early years.'

*   *   *

It was strange hearing someone else clattering around in his kitchen. Cass had insisted on making tea. Finn had accused her of being a typical Brit. Always a pot of tea in a crisis. Jokes and teasing designed to lighten the mood. Had it been a good idea telling her his past? He didn't know. It had all spilled out of him when he saw his storeroom decimated. Cass was the perfect listener. She didn't judge. He might feel a bitterness towards his mother but that didn't mean he liked others to do so. Cass had listened in the right places, softly squeezed his fingers and now she'd removed herself to do practical tasks while he composed himself mentally.

Finn turned the furniture back up the right way and replaced the cushions, those that weren't damaged. It was going to take days to right the place. He heard the tap running in the kitchen. It was good not to be alone. The thought surprised him. Usually he loved his own company here. He hated interruptions to the focus of his work. He'd turn off his mobile and disconnect the landline. He wouldn't answer the doorbell. But now. Well, he liked having Cass there.

He hardly ever brought women back to his home. He preferred to keep his assignations at a luxury hotel over a weekend or to go back to the woman's apartment. It kept his life segmented the way he wanted it. Finn shrugged. He was making too much of it. Cass wasn't here because they were lovers. She was here to do her job. And the job for the next few days for both of them was going to be clearing up this place. Finn grimaced.

'Here's a mug of brew,' Cass said,

shoving a steaming cup towards him.

'Thanks, I think. You do know we like iced tea here, especially at the height of a New York summer?'

'Oh.' She looked dismayed.

He fought the urge to kiss her lightly to counteract his teasing. She rallied after a moment and smiled sweetly.

'Back in Blighty, we love hot tea all year round. Cheers.'

'Touché.' Finn grinned and drank the stuff. It wasn't too bad, considering.

Then he put the mug down and struck one palm to the other, workman-like.

'Right, let's make a list of what needs to be done.'

★　★　★

Cass rinsed the mugs and put them down carefully on the gleaming metal draining board. It was placed next to a large sink with a complicated hot and cold water tap that looked like it cost the earth. In fact everything in Finn's kitchen looked expensive and new. And unused. Did the guy never cook?

She took a good, long moment to look around. Finn didn't require her presence right then. He had ordered her away, in fact, as he wanted to go on the computer and get his database up and running before they tackled the tumbled boxes in the spare room. So she'd suggested she tidy up in the rest of the house and he'd nodded, not really listening.

The kitchen walls were entirely bare. They were painted an attractive eggshell blue but there were no pictures, no ornaments of any kind. Cass thought of her own kitchen back in London. It was small, like the rest of her tiny rented flat. But she had adorned it with ceramic tiles, pretty chopping boards too nice to cut veg on and, of course, she had the traditional hanging garlic string.

The burglar hadn't bothered to damage the kitchen. All the damage appeared to be in the living room and the storeroom. She didn't know about the bedroom. Or should that be plural? It gave her a funny feeling thinking about where Finn slept. Which led right on to where she was going to sleep. She'd better hope he had a second bedroom. Or what?

Don't go there. If it came to it, he had a perfectly good sofa. Except that its furnishings were ripped and the filling was spread all over the floor. Cass stopped her imagination right there. She was here to work, not to fantasise about her new boss.

She opened cupboards searching for the makings of a meal. They had to eat sometime even if her body clock was all over the place. She found a cereal packet which was out of date and of a kind she'd never heard of. It brought it home to her forcefully how far away from London she was. How far from her comfort zone. She did a quick mental check of herself. She wasn't scared and she wasn't anxious. That had to be a first. She knew why.

Somehow when she was with Finn, she felt okay. It was as if the sight of his big body gave her strength. Like he was protecting her. Which was ridiculous.

Whatever it was, when she was with him, she didn't feel like hiding from the world. He had opened up to her too in a big way. Cass thought of what he'd told her about his childhood and her heart went out to him. He had spoken about it plainly but he had suffered growing up. He told his story the way she told hers. Without overt emotion. Just a set of steps from the past to the present without the colours. Cass had seen between the lines though. She saw the young Finn struggling to keep the family together despite his dysfunctional mother. Her suicide must have devastated him. Yet he'd turned into a good man and a successful one too. In spite of everything that had happened to him.

Cass gave up on the search for edibles. Finn either hadn't been home for months or he never ate. They'd have to order out or one of them would have to go food shopping. She went through to tell him so. She had to go out of the kitchen and through the wide, bright hallway to the stairs. She noticed that there were very few personal touches in Finn's house generally. For a photographer, there was a real scarcity of framed shots. Okay, he might not have many of his early childhood but hadn't he talked about living with his brothers and an Aunt later on? No family groupings to check with that. No shots of his brothers or of himself. Cass wandered into the living room to see if the photos were all clustered there. She hadn't taken much in initially apart from the violent damage.

The walls in there were quite bare too. Except for a single silver-framed photo on the far wall. She went over to see it, curiously. It was a head and shoulders shot of a stunningly beautiful young woman taken in black and white. She had high cheekbones, full sensual lips and raven hair. Cass knew without a doubt that it was Finn's mother. She felt immeasurably sad to think of how Margaret Conway's own life story had ended. There was no hint of mortality in the alluring smile and flashing dark eyes.

She ran up the stairs, glad to escape to the present day.

'Hey,' she said softly.

Finn glanced up at her from the computer he'd been frowning at. He smiled and it was like a punch to her midriff. The little crooked dip of dimple beside his mouth, the dark blue of his gaze and the dark stubble on his jaw all sent her pulse racing. She gave a little cough, instinctive displacement behaviour.

'Umm, I was going to nip out and get some food for us. Can you tell me where your nearest food shop is?'

Finn's frown was back in place but this time it was for her.

'You don't need to do that. Once I've saved this file, I'll take a break and we can order in.'

'Oh, I just thought . . . '

Then it struck her. He didn't think she could manage it. He didn't trust her to be able to find a food store, buy staples and then find her way back to his house with any confidence. The image of Finn's mother's portrait flashed into her mind. Cass's whole body went cold. Margaret Conway had been scarred and had gone on to become a dependent alcoholic and eventually to kill herself. Cass too was scarred, even if for a quite different reason. Did he think . . . ? Did Finn believe that Cass was capable of sliding down so low that she became mentally unbalanced like his mother? That she was so fragile a person that in time, she would shatter?

She turned on her heel, ignoring his concerned shout, and ran back down the stairs. She felt light-headed. She crumpled onto the bottom step. She wasn't sure what to do.

# 7

Finn didn't bother saving his file. He took one look at Cass's stricken expression and was already on his feet when she fled from him down the stairs.

'What is it? What's the matter, Cass?' He sat beside her on the stair.

'I'm not like your mother.' Cass's voice was so low he had to bend in towards her to hear.

'I never said you were.' He was taken aback. Where the heck had this come from?

'But you thought it. I know you did.' She looked at him accusingly. 'You think because I choose to lead a quiet life that I can't cope with the new.' She put the emphasis on 'choose' and 'new'.

'You're putting words into my mouth,' Finn said, starting to feel angry.

He didn't need this. She simply stared at him until he broke contact and looked at his feet. Okay. He knew what she was getting at. He was concerned about her going off on her own in the city when she didn't know the place. She had interpreted it to mean that she thought he didn't trust her to manage. He hadn't meant it like that but she was right that he thought her fragile. His Mom had appeared to be a mentally healthy individual too until the acid attack and its aftermath.

'You're wrong about me,' Cass said, 'I'm stronger than I look. I've chosen to lead my life a certain way but that doesn't mean it's the wrong way.'

'What if it is? What if it is the wrong way?' Finn asked harshly. 'The first moment I met you, I saw a beautiful woman trying to disappear into the edges of the room, to avoid being seen. You told me you gave up your language studies after the accident and after you left your fiancé. You hide your arms even though the scars aren't that bad.

You appear to have had a dead-end job until you went to France. You've given up on life.'

Cass visibly flinched but Finn held resolute. She needed to hear it. Who else was going to tell her? Lila? He doubted that Lila cared about Cass as much as she cared about herself. It was her self-centred approach to life that had drawn him to Lila. A woman who wouldn't need anything from him emotionally. So very different from her sister.

Cass didn't speak for a long while and Finn began to think he'd gone too far. Eventually he broke the silence.

'I'm sorry. It isn't my place to tell you how to lead your life. Forget what I said. And here, I'll give you a roll of dollars. There's a store on the next block where you can buy some essentials.'

'Wait.' Just one word but he froze.

'You're right. I've been a coward for the past five years.' Cass's mouth twisted. 'I've taken the easy route trying to avoid being hurt. I rent a tiny flat in a quiet part of London and I never go out in the evenings. I work at rubbishy jobs that don't need any part of the real me. I gave up on my studies because I was depressed after leaving Tom but I never resumed them because . . . I didn't have any confidence left in myself.'

Cass sighed. It was a painful intake of breath. Finn wanted to hold her and tell her it was alright but he held back. She had to get it out of her system.

'I'm fairly certain I'm not going to start drinking and end up so depressed that I can't see a reason to keep on living. Can you believe that?'

Now she gazed at him with intensity, as if willing him to believe. He nodded. He was willing to try. He didn't want to examine why it should be so important to him that Cass won through. She was, after all, only his temporary employee. A very gorgeous one, for sure, but once Liz recovered then Cass would be gone, back to London.

'I'll believe it if you prove it to me.' The words left his mouth before his mind could process them.

No wonder she looked puzzled. He wasn't too certain what he was doing either.

'How would I prove it?'

'You promise to come out to dinner with me tonight. Tomorrow we take a picnic to Central Park. The day after that, we . . . we find a museum or take a boat trip to Staten Island or whatever. The whole point is that you go out and live a little. What do you say?'

Cass laughed. It was unexpected and tinkling like summer raindrops. He grinned foolishly.

'Okay, you're on. But what about all this?' She gestured at his ruined home. 'That's why we're here, isn't it?'

It didn't seem so important right now. Finn wanted to grab Cass and run out into the city right that second while she was laughing and happy. He wanted to see her relax. She was right though. When he thought of his storeroom it brought his spirits down with a bump.

'We'll do both,' he told her. 'We work mornings to clean up and catalogue. Afternoons we party. Evenings . . . '

'Evenings we make up on our work time or if we've been good and on schedule, we go out to eat,' Cass finished, mocking him gently about his need for scheduling and timetabling.

'Right.' Finn leaned in and kissed her on the lips briefly. 'It's a pact.'

'That was just you being friendly, wasn't it?'

It had been an impulse. The touch of her soft mouth had left his lips tingling. Bad idea.

'Friends,' he agreed, a little hoarsely.

He leapt off the stair fast so she couldn't react.

'If we're going out to dinner, I must get on with sorting my files. Loads to do. Why don't you go pick a restaurant? There's a list of my favourites in the kitchen by the phone.'

'Why doesn't that surprise me? You love lists.' Cass sauntered away from him, her hips swaying just enough that he couldn't pull his gaze from them. Her jeans clung in all the right places that was for sure.

Finn took the stairs two at a time back up to the computer. It was weird but he felt energised, like a school kid on the first day of the vacation. Anticipating good things to come. He couldn't wait to take Cass out to dinner at his local Italian. He guessed she'd go for it. If she hadn't then he was sure he could persuade her to change her mind.

★   ★   ★

'French? You chose a French restaurant?' Finn asked incredulously.

'French, but in the American style,' Cass agreed, 'looking at the size of the portions.'

The waiter swooped in with menus and filled their water glasses.

'You didn't like my Italian place?'

Cass laughed, 'Don't sound so glum. You told me you eat there regularly when you're in New York. So it's good for you to try something different. Besides, if I've to prove to you that I can cope with life, then how about you prove to me that you can thrive without your scheduling?'

She looked good, Finn thought. No, that was a lie. She looked fantastic. The candlelight glinted off her pale hair and caught the shine of her eyes. She was dressed in a lacy blue dress that showed her curves. He noted the lacy sleeves and approved. Cass was making an effort for him. She wasn't entirely showing off her arms but she had moved on from hiding them behind thick cotton.

He had to admit she'd chosen the restaurant well. It was small and cosy and filled with enticing smells of garlic and freshly baked bread. He'd been there once or twice before but by himself. It was so much better to be there with Cass as his dining companion.

'So, what do you want to order?' he

asked, trying to get back on track. Staring at Cass was a pastime he could indulge in all evening but he shouldn't. It was getting harder to remember the reasons why not.

'I don't know,' Cass said honestly.

She narrowed her gaze, reading the tiny writing on the menu and shrugged.

'You've been here before. What would you recommend?'

'Let's be bold and order dishes we've never eaten before. How about squid or octopus?' Finn suggested wickedly.

She shuddered a little but nodded, 'Okay, let's go for it.'

'Really?' He'd been absolutely sure she'd wouldn't agree to it. He swallowed. Rubbed his finger on one eyebrow and looked up to see Cass grinning.

'What?'

'Oh, I don't know. You're looking a bit green round the gills. Speaking of which, do you think octopuses and squids have gills?' Cass said innocently.

Finn scowled just to see her smile

again. Her smile brightened her whole face and seemed to animate her whole body. She needed to smile more, he thought. They'd smile a whole lot in the next few days, he vowed.

The waiter arrived and they ordered a baby octopus salad for starter, followed by steaks in pepper sauce and a side order of fried squid. Cass giggled as Finn read their choices out, dead pan, as if they were a couple who adored eating invertebrates above all else.

It struck Finn that he and Cass were flirting. Lightly, but it was there all the same. It was something to do with the intimate atmosphere of the restaurant, he told himself. That, and maybe a release of tension from leaving his devastated house after hours of cleaning and sorting.

Whatever it was, he was enjoying it. And Cass looked happy too. He filled her wine glass and raised his own in a toast.

'To living life to the full.' He clinked

her glass gently with his own.

She hesitated then clinked his. 'Life to the full,' she echoed and her gaze caught his.

For a moment, it was as if the air stilled and the seconds froze on the clock. Then there was a loud crash somewhere in the back of the restaurant where the kitchens were and someone clapped and shouted. The moment was lost and the octopus salad was put in front of them and the waiter made a big deal of laying out the cutlery and changing the spoons. The evening progressed but every so often, Finn was drawn back to that moment and savoured it without quite knowing what it meant.

'I phoned Lila to tell her I'm in New York,' Cass said, prodding uncertainly at her food.

'How did she react?' Finn asked, trying a mouthful of his, and finding it not too bad.

He didn't actually care how Lila felt about Cass being in New York with him but for Cass's sake he felt he ought to at least ask the question. He had no desire to see Lila again. As far as he was concerned, their brief affair was just that. Brief and finished. It was a safe bet she had already replaced him in any case.

'She was a bit quiet at first, when I told her,' Cass said, putting down her fork and taking a sip of water. 'Then she asked me if I knew what I was doing.'

'And do you?' he asked.

It was meant to be an innocuous question as part of their casual conversation but suddenly the words stuck in his throat. Suddenly it *mattered* what she replied. Was she happy? Was she glad to be here with him?

'I know that right now, at this very minute, there's nowhere I'd rather be,' Cass said in a low voice that enveloped him in its sweetness.

When he first met her, her voice reminded him of honey. It hadn't changed. His blood ran faster in his veins and he couldn't look away from her.

★ ★ ★

She was telling the truth. There was nowhere else she'd rather be than sitting right there in a French restaurant in New York City with Finn. There was a magical element to the evening. Was it perhaps the candlelight in the restaurant which softened all the edges and gave a warm yellow glow to everything? Or was it the intensity of Finn's stare until he turned it away from her and poured more wine?

Cass had been nervous getting ready to go out. She'd laid out all Lila's dresses in the spare bedroom Finn had shown her to. It turned out he not only had a spare bedroom but that it was spacious and had the most amazing view along the street to the ever taller skyline buildings beyond.

Lila hadn't been too happy to hear

that her wardrobe wasn't arriving back in London. Cass had quickly promised to parcel up her sister's clothes and send them air freight but Lila had sulkily refused, telling her she would put up with what she had left. Cass knew Lila loved shopping so it was likely she hadn't left her with the bare necessities. Lila probably had another suitcase worth of clothes remaining in her closet, which she wasn't telling Cass about.

No, she got the strongest impression that Lila's grumpiness was more to do with the fact that Cass was with Finn. But when she tried to ask whether Ant was still on the scene, Lila blocked her and swerved the conversation away by telling her about Mandy's café and her financial troubles.

After she put the phone down, she'd deflected her worries about Lila by puzzling at her selection of clothes. She wanted to show Finn that she could go out for an evening and not hide away. On the other hand, she wasn't ready to show off her arms, no matter what he said about the scars being not too bad.

She settled on a marine-blue lacy dress and strappy shoes with kitten heels. The dress was short, skimming her thighs and she tugged it down as much as possible. She wanted to appear confident to Finn but didn't want to send out the wrong signals. She wasn't trying to impress him in *that* way. She left her hair long and free, simply brushing it until it was smooth and silky. Her makeup was minimal and she put on a dab of perfume. It was her only scent bottle. She hadn't realised she'd be away from home for longer than a couple of days.

When she went downstairs, her stomach was fluttering. Did she look as if she'd tried too hard? Or as if she hadn't tried hard enough? Finn's quirked brow and then his slow smile had calmed her nerves. She'd passed muster.

He had dressed up too. He wore charcoal trousers and a white shirt and casual jacket. It suited his rugged looks. He had shaved but there was still a shadow on his jaw which made her stomach begin to flutter once more for quite different reasons.

So, here they were. Cass's choice of eating place. She was secretly amused that he'd argued with her on the way out. He wanted to go to his Italian restaurant that he swore by for amazing food and service. She almost gave in to him but then remembered Commander Finn and decided it would do him no good to get his own way. She told him that too. He gave in good-humouredly in the end. Now it looked like he was enjoying where they were eating, as much as she was.

She had even flirted with him. It happened so naturally, she hadn't deliberately set out to do so. Somehow, it seemed safe with him. Or so she told herself, until she'd locked gazes with him as they toasted each other and waves of sensation rippled through her. It was a relief when someone smashed a plate in the restaurant kitchens and broke the mood.

'I'm going to get myself an octopus farm,' Finn said.

'Pardon?'

'I love octopus. It's a revelation to me. So, the only way to get enough is to have my own farm.'

'Do they get on well with squid? Or do you have to keep them in separate pens?' Cass asked, in the spirit of silliness.

'Here comes our main, with the fried squid side order. I won't know if I'll have squid on the farm until I've tasted it.'

The waiter slid their warmed plates in front of them with effortless skill and retreated. Around them the room buzzed with conversations and laughter and the aromas of good food wafted on the air.

'I suddenly realise what I've been missing out on,' Cass said quietly.

'Good,' Finn said. 'That's the point of this evening. You can't hide from the world forever, Cass. I won't let you. This is just the start. By the time you leave New York you'll forget staying in on evenings and wallflowering at parties. Trust me.'

*Trust me.* And she did. Finn might be bossy and over-scheduled and prone to military tidiness but she felt instinctively that he was trustworthy. She shivered. He wouldn't let her hide from the world. That was his promise. Yet in the same uttering, he had reminded her that she'd leave New York. Of course. Liz wouldn't be out of action forever and Cass was only standing in for her. She would have to leave. Leave the city. Leave Finn.

The squid didn't taste so good. She pushed it aside with her knife.

'It's an acquired taste. Bit rubbery,' Finn said, noticing.

But that wasn't it. She had a sour taste in her mouth but it was because she was going to have to leave him. It was as if someone had reached into her chest cavity and squeezed her heart.

Then she reminded herself that Finn was a man in control of his emotions who had made it clear he disliked fragility in any form. She was pretty sure she was going to miss him. But would he miss her?

A tall, willowy brunette brushed past their table with a murmured apology. Her admiring gaze caught on Finn and she smiled flirtatiously. With a fast reflex action, Finn caught the wine glass that had tipped. Cass watched as he brushed the girl's even more profuse apologies away. He was charming and polite and she had no idea how to read his expression. Was he attracted to the brunette? Who was clearly pulling out all the stops and ignoring Finn's dinner partner entirely.

'Excuse me,' Cass murmured.

Ignoring his concern, she half stumbled on her heels through the narrow gaps between the tables and into the ladies' powder room. In the large, gilt-framed mirror she saw a thin woman with large, worried eyes and a dress which showed patches of taut, pink skin on her upper arms where the lacy material had stretched and moved. She clenched her fists and beat them on the vanity top.

All of a sudden she despised the dress, the shoes, the attitudes she'd bought into tonight. This wasn't her. Who was she kidding? She was trying to be someone she wasn't. Trying to be someone that Finn Mallory would admire.

# 8

Finn didn't know what had gone wrong. They'd been having fun, or he thought they had. But something had changed. Cass was still going through the motions of eating out and conversing but now it was like her heart wasn't in it. He scrolled back mentally to try to figure out what had happened. What had he told her? *This is just the start. By the time you leave New York you'll forget staying in on evenings*. It didn't seem enough to make her stiffen into the polite but distant companion across the table from him right now. He was promising her a great few days in his favourite city and yet somehow it had all gone askew. Unless she was still scared. He was asking a lot of her in the short space of a few days.

The thing was, tonight he felt he'd seen the real Cass for the first time. The woman she would have been before her terrible accident. The woman she could be again. With Finn to help her. Why that should be so important to him, he didn't question. He was good at setting projects up, setting goals and achieving them. Maybe he couldn't help himself. Cass's future happiness was a project in itself.

Finn wasn't going to give up on her. He made that promise while they finished up their desserts and he paid the bill. He only wished she trusted him enough to tell him what was on her mind.

'Want to walk home?' he suggested as they put on their jackets and thanked the hovering waiter.

'Yes, I think I need to after that large meal,' Cass smiled.

He felt a flood of relief. She had come back to him. Her smile was genuine and she'd perked up and no longer seemed distant.

'Great. This'll let you see the city lit up at night. New York at its best. A city

148

that never sleeps.'

'Are you going to burst into song now?' she teased.

Finn took her arm in his as they swung out into the warm New York night. It felt natural to do so and she didn't pull away. Better yet, she nestled a little in towards him as if she too felt it was perfect and right.

A little voice in the back of his head was warning him off. Get outa this territory, it screamed. The lines between temporary employee and desirable woman were blurring dangerously. Finn ignored his conscience. Just for tonight, it was okay. Hey, they liked each other's company. That didn't mean he was going to take her to bed.

The images conjured up by his last thought had him heating up. If Cass was a different woman, he might act on it. But she wasn't. And he had no intention of hurting her. She'd been hurt enough in the past. He was good at self-control. He excelled at it. So why was it so difficult not to feel a prickling along his skin as her body swayed gently against his as they walked along the sidewalk?

'Thank you for dinner,' Cass said. 'It reminded me how much I used to enjoy eating out. We . . . my parents, Lila and I used to go out for a meal every Friday night when we were growing up. It was like a family ritual. Dad said it was good for us to learn our table manners and to learn how to eat nicely in front of other people. He used to say it was excellent experience for when we had careers that needed business suppers, that kind of thing.'

She laughed, but there was no bitterness in it, simply warmth, to Finn's ears.

'Poor Dad, he had no idea that neither of his daughters were going to be high fliers.'

Finn tucked her arm to his side with a squeeze that was meant to comfort.

'I didn't want to remind you of painful memories,' he said, glancing sideways at her profile and feeling a swift instinct to brush her long hair from her cheek, the better to see her sweet face.

'That's just it,' Cass exclaimed, stopping so abruptly he had to do likewise.

She looked up at him and her expression was animated. The street, the rushing heat of the night air, the sounds of vehicles and people around them all vanished from Finn's vision. All he could see was the loveliness of Cass's features as she sought to explain.

'For so long, when I've thought about them . . . about Mum and Dad . . . it's been like sticking a knife into a raw wound, so sensitive that I shut it all down. I . . . shut them out completely. It's made me feel so awfully guilty but I couldn't do it. I couldn't think about them without seeing the fire and the smoke and feeling that sense of helplessness when I couldn't save them.'

She paused. Finn didn't speak or

move. This was important. He wanted to hear what Cass had to say. She took a deep breath and went on.

'But tonight all the memories are *good*. I can see them and hear them and it's funny and tender but not too sad.'

Finn didn't think. That was the problem. He acted on impulse and he leaned right in and kissed her softly on the lips. Part of it was his happiness that she'd made an emotional breakthrough and that he had been the catalyst. Part of it . . . he just wanted to kiss her. Her lips tasted of vanilla ice-cream from dessert and sweetly quintessentially of Cass. He half expected her to push him away so it was a surprise when her mouth mobilised under his, her lips parting and allowing his tongue to seek hers.

Finn forgot all his wise promises not to mix business with pleasure. Forgot that Cass was not the sort of woman he should be tempting or be tempted by. He gave himself up to the joy of kissing

her as his mouth hardened over hers
and demanded more.

* * *

Cass kissed him back, giving as much
passion to it as he was. Her body was
on fire with her need for him and she
pressed against him, feeling the hard-
ness of his body. He wanted her too.
They couldn't pretend this was a kiss
between two friends. There was raw
passion enclosing them, their body
electricity zapping the air.

Who stopped first? Her head was so
dizzy with her excitement for him, Cass
didn't know. She only knew she was so
strongly and deeply attracted to Finn
that she was never going to find her way
out. And she didn't want to.

Her chest was heaving as they made a
small gap between their bodies. Her
body ached for his. She had to be
reasonable, Cass thought. She knew he
didn't love her. She knew he was the
sort of man who took lovers as

short-term relationships only. His work was his passion. He had his own personal demons from his childhood and she understood why he didn't want to get involved. Especially with a woman like her. But none of that had mattered right in the midst of that kiss. Besides, wasn't he the one who had started it?

Finn took her hand in his large, warm one as they walked together round the corner of the block to his house. For some reason, that tender gesture was almost her undoing. It wasn't the intense, searing passion of a kiss. It was togetherness, comfort and solid trust.

You're overthinking this, she warned herself. Remember Lila. Had Finn acted like this with Lila? Did he do this with every woman he had a whim for? They didn't speak as they went up the steps and into the house. Cass felt awkward. What was he thinking? Did he regret kissing her? She couldn't tell from his expression. He was busy flicking on the light switches so that the room was cast cosily with lamplight.

'Coffee?' Finn called from the kitchen.

'Yes, lovely, thanks. I'll come and help.' Cass went to join him.

They were acting politely as if nothing had happened. The kitchen seemed all of a sudden too small. They kept bumping into each other and apologising. Their fingers touched over the coffee pot and fled back fast. His touch burned her. She didn't want coffee anyway. She couldn't bear the suspense in the atmosphere.

'What was that?' she burst out.

For an awful second, she thought he was going to pretend he didn't know what she was talking about. But she had misjudged him. Finn sighed, put the cream container down.

'Do you want me to apologise?'

'No,' she said, horrified. 'We both were party to it.'

'It'. Come on, Cass. Say the word. *Kiss*.

'But I kissed you first,' he argued, 'so

that makes it my fault.'

'Don't be ridiculous,' Cass said, 'I kissed you right back.'

His gaze flickered over her mouth and she felt that tingle of heat start up all over.

'What do you want this to be?' he asked softly.

'I . . . I don't know,' she lied.

She was utterly confused about what she wanted. They liked each other, right? But was that enough? Was that sufficient basis on which to start an affair? Could she take a risk? She didn't know if she was strong enough emotionally unless they were both committed. Which they weren't.

'I can't promise you anything,' Finn said, echoing her thoughts. 'We both know there's a major physical attraction between us. There has been since we met at the Biarritz party. The moment I kissed you, thinking you were Lila. The question is, do we act on it? Cass?'

Why can't you promise me anything?

she wanted to ask, petulantly. Why not? She already knew the answer to that. She was wrong for him. So, now she had a choice. She could have a brief and physical love affair with him or they could agree that this whole thing was a mistake. Pretend like it never happened.

She shook her head. She knew the answer before she even mulled it over. Cass Bryson was cautious and risk free. She wasn't the sort to have a wild and abandoned affair. Not unless her heart and his were committed. If only she were more like Lila.

'I can't.'

She couldn't even attempt to explain why not. How making love to him would rip out her heart when there was no love involved between them. She didn't know if she was capable of offering love. Not after what had happened with Tom. So it shouldn't have hurt to see a look of relief on his face. Besides, how would he react when she took off her clothes and he had to see the scarring? She couldn't bear to witness his disgust. No, it was much, much safer to stay away from him.

'Agreed,' Finn said, as if they were in a business meeting and had come to the point of deal closure. His voice was brisk and emotionless and it made her want to cry. It didn't mean much to him if he could dust it off so lightly. He'd probably realised he didn't want her, damaged as she was. So she was giving him an easy 'out'.

'Let's have that coffee now,' Cass said lightly.

Two could play the game of not caring. She wasn't going to let him see her misery. She was a grown-up. She could act as if discussing having an affair and deciding on balance, not to, was an everyday event. She could be as worldly as him.

They took their drinks through to the living room and sat on the floor cushions. The soft furnishings with their spilled-out stuffing were stacked in the cellar awaiting the trash collection. It was difficult to keep a mental and real dignified space from Finn when sprawling on a colourful cushion, Cass thought wryly.

Finn looked awkward too. His legs were too long and his upper body too broad, to be sitting comfortably on his own floor.

'First thing tomorrow, I'm going shopping for a new suite,' he said, slopping the coffee accidentally.

'I could help with that,' Cass offered tentatively, desperate for them to get back onto a harmonious footing. 'I decorated my flat in London and friends have told me they liked it.'

'I could use your help,' he said easily, 'I'm colour blind when it comes to matching up furnishings.'

'What about our Central Park picnic? Should we put it on hold?'

'We'll do both.'

'What about cataloguing?' Cass reminded him. 'It isn't finished, by a long chalk.'

Finn stretched out his long legs and

began to look more at home on the floor. He shoved an extra cushion behind him and leaned back, relaxed. Cass shifted her own position so that her hip bones weren't screaming from hitting the polished wood. Finn threw a small cushion to her and she caught it and wedged it between herself and the armchair.

They were okay with each other again. She let out a breath slowly and a layer of tension with it. Finn was grinning.

'What?'

'I can't help picturing you as a mermaid. It's the way you naturally sit, with your legs tucked up to the side. Have you ever visited the Little Mermaid in Denmark?'

Cass shook her head. It brought home yet again the gulf that existed between their two lives. Finn was so well-travelled.

'You should go see her. It's a marvellous sculpture. Anyway, it's whimsical of me, I know, but I imagine photographing you like that.' His eyes took on a light as if an idea had switched on. 'Remember when we went swimming at Sylvia's beach? You swam like a mermaid. If I could capture that on film . . . '

'What about your Hidden Places project?' Cass interrupted. 'And sorting out your database here. Not to mention all the cleaning and repairs still to be done.'

'You're no fun,' Finn said lazily. 'Here I am, coming up with creative ideas and all you can do is pour cold water on them. For shame.'

'Commander Finn,' Cass said.

'And that is who, exactly?' Finn quirked an eyebrow mildly.

Cass flushed. She hadn't meant to speak out loud.

'It's my name for you,' she confessed. She held up her palm before he could reply. 'Or it was. I coined it when I was in the plane flying to France. Everything was so perfectly in its place and your pilot told me you like everything to be in order, shipshape. When I met you, you didn't do anything to change my opinion.'

She sneaked a glance at him over the rim of her mug. Was he mad with her? With relief, she saw he was grinning. Then he laughed right out loud and Cass couldn't help but join in.

'I'm sorry,' she said, wiping her eyes from the laughter. 'It was very rude of me.'

'Not at all,' Finn said, 'I quite like it. It sums me up.'

'I'm not so sure,' Cass smiled, indicating his reclined posture. 'You don't look like the Commander right at this minute.'

'What do I look like?' His voice honeyed.

The tiny hairs on her arms sprang up, shivering. They couldn't get away from it. This mysterious pull that drew them together.

'Oh, I don't know,' she said airily, 'Finn McCool?'

The truth was, she felt like she was

seeing the real Finn tonight. Not the tightly controlled man who had everything just so, ordered and tabled the way he wanted it. The real Finn who was charming and honest and fun to be with.

Finn snorted. 'Finn McCool? Isn't that some mythical warrior in Celtic legends?'

'Oh, is it? I just meant that you are different this evening. You're relaxed and I think you're enjoying yourself. Am I right?'

'The company of a beautiful woman, a delicious French meal out and my hard wooden floor to sit on. What's not to like?'

'You're teasing me,' Cass said, making a face at him.

He was teasing her and she was enjoying it far too much. They were going to get back to reality the next day with a major bump. There were too few days to get it all sorted before she had to leave. Talk about pouring cold water. That took her down like lead weights on a line.

'What's the matter?' Finn asked.

He was very tuned to her moods tonight, Cass realised. They were getting along so well. Too well. There could be no more kissing, no more getting close.

'I was thinking of all the work we need to make up tomorrow,' she said truthfully.

'Yeah, well, tomorrow is another day. Talking of which,' Finn stood and flexed his shoulders ruefully, 'I'm going to turn in now. You got all you need for the spare room?'

Cass stood too. He was at least a foot taller than her and so much broader. If he wanted to, he could pick her up. Just like the mythical Celtic warrior. She hid a smile. He wasn't the only one who could be whimsical.

'Good night, Cass.' Finn spoke quietly. He waited momentarily, then with a nod, he went out of the room and she heard his footsteps on the stairs.

She had not dared to read his emotions. She went up to the spare bedroom and sat on the edge of the bed. Tiredness hit her like a hammer. She pulled off Lila's dress and caught sight of her body in the mirror. She smoothed her fingers slowly over the scars. She was right to have turned Finn down.

They may have enjoyed each other's company that evening and had fallen into a friendship, but being so close was dangerous. His kisses were dangerous. She could fall so very readily into a situation where she would get hurt.

She had to remember that this was all transient. Liz must surely be recuperating out there on the other side of the Atlantic, in Biarritz. She should remind Finn tomorrow to phone and find out. She hoped Liz was getting better, for her sake. She also wanted to know how many days were left. Before she had to give Finn Mallory up for ever.

# 9

New York was incredible. Cass gawped at the enormously tall buildings, their windows glinting in the sharp sunlight. The gaudy billboards the size of a house posted on every surface, the neon signs just as huge, bold and brassy advertising all manner of eats and objects, places and people. The yellow cabs zooming down the long, endless grey streets. The stream of crowds on every sidewalk. It was heady and exotic and she felt carefree as she and Finn joined the rest of humanity, on the way to the furniture store.

The heat seared her and she lifted the hem of her cotton shirt to waft in some air. It was quite a different heat from that of Biarritz and she compared them, then grinned.

'What ya thinking?' Finn smiled down at her.

'I'm thinking how well travelled I've got recently. So nice to be able to compare the climates of an American eastern seaboard city with that of a west coast French city and to have personally visited both within the week.'

'Now you see why I like travelling so much,' Finn said. 'The photography is just an excuse to mosey about all over our small world.'

'Small?'

He shrugged. 'Yeah, small. Seriously, once you get the travel bug you realise it's not so far from America to England or from Japan to Australia.'

'It helps if you can afford it, of course,' Cass said.

'True, but that's not why you don't travel, is it?'

She winced. He didn't dress it up.

'No, you know why I don't go places,' she admitted. 'I don't like the idea that I might get mixed up in stuff I can't handle.'

'Like what?' He sounded genuinely curious.

'I don't know . . . like getting mugged or knocked down by a train far from home or . . . or dying of a disease in the tropics.' She flung up her arms to encompass all that could go wrong with the world and was annoyed when Finn simply laughed.

'Cass, you could as easily get mugged in your own street in London or get knocked down by a bus or train there too. The tropical disease, not so much but you could get ill at home. Don't you think you're trying for excuses?'

'I suppose nothing terrible has happened since I got on the plane to Biarritz.'

Nothing terrible, only life-changing. Getting employed by a rugged traveller-photographer who, every time she looked at him, made her heart pump faster. Besides, hadn't the worst already happened when fire broke out at her childhood home? She couldn't be so unlucky in the rest of her life surely? Which was a new way to think, she mused.

'There you go then,' Finn said triumphantly, in response to her previous admission.

She stuck her tongue out at him childishly but he only grinned and gave her a quick hug. They jumped away immediately. She wasn't the only one to be aware of the 'no go' invisible sign between them, then.

'Here we are,' Finn said, not looking at her.

He pushed open the door to a large store and Cass followed him in. It was the most enormous sales floor she had ever seen. Like the size of a small country. There were beds and chairs, sofas and armchairs, sideboards and what she would call Welsh dressers, although she guessed the Americans might label them differently.

'Impressive,' she said.

'Or horrific, depending on your view point,' Finn grimaced.

'You don't like shopping?' Cass said, pretending to be shocked.

'You do?' he countered.

'I love it. Mind you, I'm more of a window shopper due to not having much cash ever.'

'Well, this is your opportunity,' Finn said. 'I want you to find me a living room suite that's tasteful and comfortable and I don't care what it costs as long as I can sit down on it and feel good.'

Cass rubbed her hands together in delight.

'Do you want to go and grab a coffee and meet me back here in an hour or two?' she suggested.

'It's gonna take that long?' Finn looked shocked now. 'I was scheduling in a half hour at most. Besides, what about our picnic? You can't get out of it when you promised me.'

'Finn, look at the size of this place. I could hardly walk from one end of the store to the other in a half hour. Seriously. You should go and get the picnic food and I'll meet you outside in a while. Synchronise watches?'

Finn was looking at her in a strange

way. Did she have a smut on her cheek? Cass ran her hands over her hot face self-consciously.

'You don't give yourself enough credit,' he said oddly. 'You're better than you realise.'

It wasn't until he'd gone that she sort of understood what he meant. Here she was, alone in a city store the size of Mars and she didn't feel scared. She touched her bag for reassurance. She had a map of the city and her phone in it along with some cash that Finn had lent her. She had insisted she would get to a bank to get her Euros changed but had seen the practicalities of borrowing from her boss in the meantime.

Besides, she didn't need to feel insecure. Finn would be back at the arranged hour and spot. She trusted him implicitly. Knowing he was about, even if he was gone a few blocks, gave her more confidence than anything else.

She felt adventurous and a little bit thrilled to be wandering around the furniture, trying to imagine it fitting into Finn's house. An assistant came over at once to ask if she wanted any help but she politely sent him away, saying she was just looking. She savoured the idea of choice. That whatever she chose for Finn, she would be able to imagine him using over the next decade. If he didn't like shopping, he was hardly likely to revamp his décor in under ten years.

A vivid purple sofa with overstuffed cushions and wooden curlicue arm rests made her think of Lila. Her sister had a penchant for purple. Her rented room, in Mandy's flat, was almost entirely shades of that colour. She wished she hadn't phoned her late last night.

Cass had been restless after she'd gone up to her bedroom. The events of the evening kept playing in her mind. The intimacy and fun of the restaurant, Finn's kisses and their decision not to have an affair. It all swirled around in her head leaving her unable to sleep.

Eventually she got up and looked at her watch, using the light from the scarlet neon sign on the opposite side of the street to see the clock face. It was two thirty in the morning. So that meant it was seven thirty in London. Lila would be up and getting ready for work. She reached for her phone and speed-dialled.

'Yes?' Lila's grumpy, morning voice. She wasn't a natural early riser.

'Hey, it's me. Good morning.'

'You phoned to say that? I have a blistering headache, and me and Ant had our first row last night. So, no, it's not a good morning at all. What do you want?'

What did she want? Cass wasn't sure. She was so mixed up right now she just wanted to hear a friendly voice. A voice from home. Lila was her older sister and Cass instinctively turned to her when she needed help. Lila didn't always give it, unless it suited her. Cass knew her sister inside out and loved her but she had no illusions about her. There was no-one else in any case. Finn. She could count on Finn. Maybe.

173

But not for this conversation.

'Cass? Are you still there? Only I haven't had my breakfast yet, I'm half dressed and I'm desperate for coffee.'

'It doesn't matter,' Cass said. 'I was feeling a bit homesick, that's all.'

'Oh, well, that's what you get for swanning off across half the world without thinking about me,' Lila said nastily.

'Thinking about you,' Cass repeated. 'What do you mean?'

'You know fine well what I mean. I mean sneaking behind my back with Finn. That's what I mean.'

'You've got Ant,' Cass said, her voice coming out too loud with irritation. She kept it quieter, aware of Finn sleeping not far away through the wall from her. 'Finn's given me the distinct impression that it's over between you and him.'

Lila made a disparaging sound.

'Oh for goodness sake, Lila. Grow up. It's not all about you,' Cass snapped.

There was a stunned silence over the line. They were both astonished then. Usually Lila got to boss Cass about and she took it. She never, but never argued back.

'Sorry,' Cass murmured. 'I shouldn't have shouted. But I don't think you should harbour any hope where Finn is concerned.'

'Let me be the judge of that,' Lila's voice came pertly down the phone. 'Anyway, if you're so homesick, give me your address and I'll send you a postcard from London.'

Cass told her the address. A postcard wasn't going to solve her situation. Why had she imagined that phoning Lila was going to help?

'I've got my own problems, thanks for asking. Mandy's café is on the brink of closing. She's losing business left, right and centre and I'll probably lose my job,' Lila was saying.

So then Cass spent the next ten minutes supporting her sister and trying to boost her spirits, alternately

commiserating and suggesting solu-
tions, none of which Lila liked. The
conversation about Lila and Finn was
not mentioned again.

Now she turned away abruptly from
the purple suite and tried not to dwell
on Lila and her problems. She promised herself that she'd find time soon to
phone Lila back and try to discuss her
future more thoroughly. She also had to
find out from Finn how many days they
were staying in New York. She really
should get back to London and help
Lila. She sighed. At the rate they were
ignoring the work in his house, they
might just be here longer than antici-
pated.

So much for Commander Finn. Cass
smiled. He didn't seem quite so on
track lately for some reason. Ironically,
she was now in the position of gently
reminding him of what they had to do.
It was her job, as his personal assistant,
to do so.

There it was. She stopped dead. The
perfect suite. It was very much bachelor

colours and style, being dark solid oak and maroon cushions, but it looked comfortable and as if it would wear well over the years. She could quite imagine Finn lounging on it. Sexily. She swallowed. Really. She had only to think of him and her body flared up. It was madness.

\* \* \*

Finn waited on the sidewalk. He looked at his wrist watch. It was almost at the time they'd agreed to meet. He had a bag full of bagels and chips and snack boxes of fruit. He didn't like shopping but he'd enjoyed thinking of what Cass would like, when he chose the food. He didn't care much what he ate. Travelling had done that. It didn't pay to be a fussy eater when scooting about over the globe on a tight schedule of shots. He liked the idea of Cass's face lighting up when she saw the ripe strawberries he'd picked and the blueberries fresh from the farm, or so the store keeper had promised.

His heart flipped when Cass came out of the store, smiling at him. The sight of her made him feel unreasonably happy. It never failed. Finn had dated many women but none of them had brought that glow to him. None of them had made him feel that deep connection when he kissed them.

Finn swallowed. He had to forget the kisses he'd shared with Cass. They had had the conversation last night in the kitchen. They had agreed there was not going to be an affair. So, no more kissing, no more body contact.

He hadn't been surprised at her answer when he asked her what she wanted their kiss to be. He'd known she wasn't the sort of woman to want a brief affair. Therefore, logically, he couldn't regret what had never occurred. But regret was what he felt, even though he knew he couldn't offer her more. It wasn't his style to start something and let it linger on. He preferred that they both knew where they stood. And he stood most definitely on the side of a short passion where no strings were attached. If it was going to happen at all.

'You are now the proud owner of a gorgeous living room suite,' Cass told him. 'Do you want to see it?'

He shook his head. 'I trust you to surprise me with something good.'

She shot him a fleeting glance with her large, expressive eyes. He'd meant the suite but it held true of other things too. She constantly surprised him in a good way. He had to force his hand away. Without thinking, he'd been reaching for hers so they could walk together to Central Park.

You're better than you realise, he'd said to her when he left her in the store. He meant it. She'd surprised him with her resilience. He had underestimated her ability to cope. Compared her instead to his mother and feared the same vulnerability and flaws. Now he had to re-evaluate his judgements and when he did, he had to admit that Cass was nothing like Margaret Conway. She was complex, yes, and she had her fears and insecurities, but there was a toughness to her that he doubted she even understood.

His cell phone buzzed. Finn took it out and scanned the texts.

'It's a message from Liz's sister. She went over to Biarritz to look after her. I asked her keep me informed with regular updates on Liz's condition.'

'How is Liz? I hope she's on the mend,' Cass said.

'She's still struggling but the pain is manageable now and she's able to get around for a short while each day without much pain, according to this report.'

'That's good news.'

'Yeah, it is. Doesn't sound like she's ready to get back to work yet though,' Finn frowned.

Cass looked away from him, her fingers laced as she asked, 'So how long will I be working for you?'

Finn stopped in the middle of the busy sidewalk as people streamed by, ignoring the grumbling as they had to step by him or bump into him.

'Are you wishing you hadn't taken the work?' Why that should hurt, he didn't know.

He had a rush of relief when she shook her head.

'No, it's not that. It's the opposite. I'm enjoying being here. Perhaps too much.' She sighed.

'Why shouldn't you enjoy your work? Better than hating it,' he grinned.

'True. I've become so used to working in dull jobs where I do hate it, I've forgotten what it is to work at something where I feel good.'

'Like your language studies,' he suggested mildly. He wondered if he'd gone too far when her brows drew together sharply.

She sighed again and pursed her lips as if she'd say nothing. Finn waited her out. She had to work it through all by herself. He couldn't do it for her, much as he might like to. He knew she was wasting her talents by not going back to her studies. She had to know it too. When she spoke again, he knew he was right about her.

'Like my language studies,' she repeated. 'You're right. I gave up on them along with everything else. What was it you said? That I'd given up on life.'

'I was too harsh,' Finn said, remembering what he'd said to her in his anger and frustration that she was wasting her life. 'It wasn't my place to say the things I did.'

'If you didn't speak them to me, then who would?' Cass said plainly, looking straight at him with wide, honest eyes.

It was as if he could dive right into their clear depths and swim to her very core. Like he could see right inside her.

'You were right,' Cass went on, 'I told you that and it's true. When my confidence crumbled I gave up on so many things. That's why this job is such a change for me. I don't wake up dreading the day, knowing I'm going to be bored out of my mind by typing letters for hours or filing reports in an office from eight until six with a break for tea and a break for lunch. Lonely breaks where I ate by myself because I didn't want to get friendly with anyone. I didn't even have the confidence to make new friends. But now . . . maybe after this, after Liz gets better and comes back to work for you, maybe I will go back to college and finish my language course.'

Cass sounded so surprised that Finn wanted to smile. Not at her but *with* her. It was like she was waking up to what her future could be. Slowly and sleepily but getting there. But at the same time, a heavy weight dropped in his stomach. He let it lie there, not understanding at first. What was dragging him down?

Liz getting better. He was very fond of Liz. She was a great assistant and more than that, she was a friend. But when she returned, Cass had to leave.

He felt a premonition of loss. That was the heaviness in his guts. He forced himself to think positive. London wasn't so far from anywhere. Hadn't he told Cass how small the world was? He had to prove it, that was all. But the feeling of let down followed him as they continued walking.

'Finn?' Cass was saying, sounding a little hurt.

He zoned back in to their conversation which obviously had halted while his head was elsewhere.

'Sorry,' he mumbled. He wished he could ditch their plan to go to the Park for a picnic. Right then, it was the last activity he wanted. What he wanted was to go home and lose himself in his cataloguing. Cass had been right when she hassled him to get working. He was half going to say so when he remembered her delight at the notion of the picnic. He didn't have the heart to spoil it for her.

'I thought you'd be pleased,' she said, 'that I'm going to go back to college.'

'It's not about pleasing me,' he said, too loudly, 'I'm just your temporary boss, remember. Another week or two, you won't even be here and neither will I. We'll probably never cross paths again.'

Finn didn't want to look at Cass's distressed face. Didn't want to see the glimmer of tears, quickly blinked away. He felt horrible. It was as if the whole day had lost its shine.

# 10

Central Park in the midst of a hot New York summer was wonderful. There were sail boats with colourful billowing cloths on the main water body and groups of picnickers, cyclists, roller-bladers and sightseers everywhere.

Cass followed Finn, willing herself to enjoy it. He was right. She wasn't going to be here long. So that meant she had to absorb all the excitement and atmosphere as much as possible to remember it all when she was back home in her tiny flat in the greyness of a London summer.

She shouldn't feel hurt that he'd reminded her of the short nature of her employment with him. He was totally right. Clearly, he didn't care whether he saw her again after that or not. Let's face it. Finn Mallory moved in completely different circles to her. She was never going to see him after this.

Even if she felt like crying inside, Cass wasn't going to show it. She wasn't going to waste these moments here with him. She was going to make the most of them, to the last drop and then take the memories and hoard them for the rest of her life. She was going to miss him and it was hopeless but she couldn't simply switch her feelings off. She didn't want to.

'What about here?' Finn asked, indicating a shallow ledge on the rocks, overlooking a huge pond.

There were other people basking on the great stones but not close. Cass nodded. It was fine. Anywhere was fine as long as she shared it with him. She sat near to him but with a fine gap so they were in no danger of accidentally touching.

Finn opened up the brown paper bag and brought out plastic tubs and totes. There was even a small paper tablecloth with bright red checks. Cass spread it out on the warm stone. It was going to be a proper picnic, she decided. She'd be chirpy and cheerful and chatty until Finn smiled at her. He was far too sombre for the sunny day. So was she.

'Mmm, strawberries, my favourite,' she said brightly, peeling the lid from the container with enthusiasm.

Finn quirked a brow. Okay, she was laying it on thick but what was the alternative? Cass imagined lying down and sobbing. That would look lovely, wouldn't it. She could just imagine Finn's puzzled expression if his assistant did that. Mind you, he looked pretty puzzled as it was, at her change of mood.

She ploughed on, regardless, willing him to play the game too.

'What else did you get? Olives, lovely. Paprika crisps, never tried that flavour but sounds good, I adore blueberries and oh, and bagels, fab.'

She smiled widely at him until he gave her a small smile back. That was better. She offered him the tub of blueberries.

'This place is much bigger than I thought it would be,' she said conversationally.

She didn't care what size Central Park was but she wanted him to speak. He had been silent too long, like he was mulling something over and didn't like his conclusions. Was he regretting asking her to fill in for Liz? Was that it? His funny mood had come on when she had started talking about work and about going back to college. When he'd reminded her that she wasn't essential to him. Not the way Liz was. That she wasn't going to see him after this was over.

She drew in a long breath. Absorbed the scents of the city summer too. It was magical here. They were right in the centre of the busy metropolis yet it was as if they were in the countryside. Beside her, Finn's shoulders dropped and he threw a handful of blueberries down his throat.

When he'd finished them, he turned to her, and Cass was pleased to see he was back to normal.

'It's three hundred hectares in size,' he said. 'It's an amazing place, isn't it?'

'I'm not sure exactly what size a hectare is,' Cass replied, 'but I can see it stretches for what seems like miles. It really is amazing.'

Finn delved into his bag and brought out his camera. He started taking shots of the sail boats and the geese pecking at the water's edge and the mallard bobbing along on the shallows. He was concentrating, his entire focus on his view finder. The muscles on his arms stood out as he turned the camera to the angles he wanted. Cass admired him for that. His single-mindedness when it came to his work. Plus she liked the sight of his muscled arms, flexing.

She had declared her intention to go back to her studies. Had felt a thrill when saying it. Now she felt trepidation as well as a longing. It was a longing to do what Finn did. To immerse in a subject that really interested her. She loved languages. She *had* loved them.

Before she lost confidence in her ability to do anything right. Could she go back and finish her studies?

He had laid the camera down now and was breaking the bread. Cass idly picked it up. She aimed it at the glittering water and a red boat that was gliding past and pressed the button. There was a triangle symbol for reviewing the images and she pressed it, curious to see what she had captured.

She had caught the sunshine glinting off the surface of the greenish water well. The boat, not so much. It was blurred. She was going to put the camera back down when Finn took it and looked at her photo.

'Not very good, is it?' Cass wrinkled her nose.

Finn smiled, 'It's not bad for a first attempt. The problem was the boat was moving so you used the wrong setting on the dial. See, you have to choose what you want in focus then get the right shutter speed. Want me to show you?'

She nodded. She did want that. Not because she was particularly interested in photography but because his eyes lit up when he discussed the subject and it warmed her too. And because, if he liked it so much, then she wanted to as well. At least to know a little about it.

'Okay,' Finn said enthusiastically, 'scoot over here and you'll get a great angle on the sailboats.'

Cass scooted. The stone was smooth and flat and she was able to crab across it to sit in front of Finn. She was immediately and far too intensely aware of his body heat as he guided her hands onto his camera. His fingertips were calloused but gentle as he laid his hands over hers on the sides of the camera and tilted it towards the boats.

She felt his breath on the top of her hair and the shell of her ear as he explained how the angle changed the frame of the picture and how important the framing was to the final image. She was listening, she was sure she was. But she wasn't sure she could repeat what he was telling her. It was too distracting, the strength of his chest leaning just so, on her back and shoulders as he tried to describe the shutter speed and why it mattered. His long legs were either side of her. His thighs brushed hers. The sensation was rippling like an underwater eddy. She tried to focus.

He demonstrated the dangers of wobble by turning the camera in their shared grasp. Showed her how to correct it with some function button somewhere on the top of the box. She had turned a little towards him and his jaw grazed her forehead with its bristling growth. It made her skin tingle and burn in the most pleasant way. His lips were firm and sculpted as he spoke, Cass thought dreamily. So close to her. She could reach out . . .

'Do you see what I mean?' Finn was asking.

'Yes, yes I do,' she said meaninglessly.

What on earth had he been telling her?

He pushed the camera at her.

'Great, well have a go. See if you can put it into practice.'

He folded his arms and grinned at her. Cass wondered suspiciously if he realised she hadn't been listening. She took the camera reluctantly and prepared for the shot.

★   ★   ★

Finn was having far too much fun. He was also being unfair to her. Finn had been distracted too by Cass's nearness. Showing her how the camera worked was a fine excuse to be close to her. The scent of delicate flowers from her hair had almost driven him wild. His lips were a hair's breadth from the small curl of her ear. Within kissing and nibbling range. They just couldn't keep away from each other, he acknowledged ruefully.

So much for the decision they had both made, not to get involved. Like strong magnets they instinctively drew together. What was worse was that his resolve was dissolving. He saw less and less reason why they shouldn't be together. She wasn't the fragile creature he'd first thought she was. There was so much more to her. Behind the sweet, delicate façade, Cass Bryson was strong in spirit and increasing in strength the more he got to know her.

It was only her firm voice telling him she couldn't have an affair that held him back. She had to want it too. Her body clearly did. But Finn wouldn't push her. It wasn't right of him.

'Okay, what do you think of that?' Her voice was pleased as she held out the camera on playback.

Finn scrutinised it carefully. She wasn't a natural with the shots but she had taken some of what he was telling her on board. The picture was a big improvement on her first shot. The sail boat was in focus and the water was blurred but in an artistic kind of way. Cass had captured the onward motion of the boat perfectly, there was a feeling of movement and energy about it that he really liked.

Just as he really liked her. Cass's face was open and bright as she waited for his opinion. Her cheeks were prettily flushed from the sun and her green eyes sparkled just as beautifully as the sparkles on the water nearby. The cotton arm of her shirt had rolled up above her elbow and the first snaking scars were just visible. He didn't think. He reached out and stroked her skin. Stroked the shined, raised welt.

Cass froze but he didn't stop. His fingers gently encircled her arm before he let his fingers drop. Turned his focus slowly to the shot.

'It's great. There's something about it.' *There's something about you.*

He began to pack up the paper bag with empty plastic tubs and the chip wrapper and the remains of the bread. His head was swirling but he hoped Cass couldn't see how confused he was. She still had his camera. She jumped up off the rocks with it and started photographing some ducks waddling towards her in the hope of a feeding.

It gave him a chance to sort out his thoughts. He liked Cass far too much. The problem was that she had been hurt by her fiancé and didn't trust another man to be attracted to her with her damage. He could overcome that obstacle. He'd never wanted another woman the way he wanted Cass. He'd show her how much he wanted her.

*Stop right there*. She wanted him too. It was obvious. That wasn't the problem. The real issue was that he was completely wrong for her. She didn't like travel. She didn't like risk. Yes, she was coping pretty well with moving firstly to France and then to America but would she want to live like that for however long their love affair lasted? Because Finn had no intention of giving up his wandering or his career to stay home.

Then there was his career. It had always come first. It was his sanctuary from chaos. Being with Cass was a distraction that'd take his time away from his photography and his projects.

He didn't have time for an affair with her. There it was. Pure and simple. Which was why he went for shallow women like Cass's sister who didn't expect more of him than a weekend. He already knew a weekend with Cass was never going to be enough.

Where was she anyway? He felt a slight panic when he couldn't see her with the family of ducks any more. She didn't know the place. She might get lost or get grabbed or . . . He let his breath out. Cass was walking back towards him from behind a jut in the rock. She was staring at the camera with a smile that lit him up.

To counter it, he was deliberately short, hating himself for being so contrary and messed up, for not knowing really what he wanted.

'We should go.'

'Okay. It's early yet though.'

He heard the hope in her voice and stamped on it ruthlessly. Knowing if he spent more time with her, his resolve would melt like ice-cream under the sun.

'You were the one told me we've too much work to do,' he said, keeping the edge to his tone. 'We should get back now.'

'You're right. We've played hooky for long enough. Thanks for the picnic, Finn, it was lovely.'

Dammit. Did she have to be so nice to him? He practically ground his teeth, trying to stay surly. He needed distance from her. Physical and mental. It was best for both of them.

He marched in front, leading the way. Ignoring her bewildered face. All he had to do was be her boss. Be polite and nice and lay out sufficient work for them so that he needn't dwell on his emotions one little bit. Perhaps he could phone Liz's sister and get her to speed Liz up on her recovery. If Liz was able to walk short distances without suffering, then surely she could get on a plane stateside pronto and help him out here. He was grasping at straws.

Behind him, he heard Cass's soft tread. When they reached the street, he had to wait for her and walk abreast. It would look strange if he continued to march ahead the way he wanted to. He was conscious of her all the way back to his house.

'Back to work then,' Cass said with a smile that didn't reach her troubled eyes.

'Back to work,' he agreed.

Now he'd reached his own door step he was looking forward to getting inside and putting the computer on to finish sorting his database. At least that way, he wouldn't have to think about his feelings for Cass.

'You prefer this to being out picnicking.' She said it as a fact.

'I seem to remember that I'm paying you a daily rate to work.'

Her words had stung him and he'd retaliated. There was no way he wanted her to know just how much he'd enjoyed their time together today. He groaned silently.

'So you are. I do apologise. I don't want to waste any more billable hours so let's get in and get started.' Her voice was icy.

Finn started to speak, then changed his mind. He shut his mouth in a grim line and unlocked the front door.

He wanted to say sorry. That he realised he was the one who'd suggested the evening out at the restaurant, the furniture shopping and the Central Park picnic. That he had persuaded her that she should go out and live a little. It wasn't her fault they were way behind on getting Finn's house back to normal. It wasn't her fault he was way behind on his Hidden Places project. Bill Hamilton was leaving messages on his cell, asking when he expected to be back to finish it. So far, Finn had given only the vaguest of answers.

But he was mixed up. He had the mother of all headaches. He blamed the searing sun but it wasn't that. It was his emotions all churned up and going nowhere. It was Cass's perfume that lingered in his nostrils as she stomped past him and into the house. It was the vision of her perfect rear clad in those slimline jeans she favoured that had his insides going like a cement mixer. It was her laughter that rang in his ears from her triumphant photography down at the Park waters.

Finn waited until the last of Cass's loud clattered steps upstairs had gone. Then he let it all out in a loud groan and he didn't care whether the whole neighbourhood heard or not.

# 11

Cass was seriously annoyed. She stood in Finn's study which was on the ground floor, off the living room. It too had been turned over by the intruder and had not yet been returned to any semblance of normality. It wasn't the state of the room or the thought of the vandals destroying it mindlessly that was making her simmer to boiling point. No, it was her boss. How dare he insinuate that she was wasting her working hours! Wasn't he the one who had suggested the outings in the first place?

Upstairs, a floorboard creaked. Finn had gone straight up to his computer, shutting the door and making it quite clear that he didn't want company. Having stormed up the stairs to show her indignance, Cass had then had to come back down to keep a haughty distance from him.

She had hesitated in the hall, unsure what to do to burn off her anger. Then, she went through the living room which was almost repaired, to the room leading off it. She hadn't been in it before and one glance was enough to see that it needed some serious work done. There was a large, dark maple wood desk overpowering the rest of the space. The books, papers and ornaments had been swept off it onto the afghan carpet. The desk drawers were open and had been rifled.

The desk chair was overturned. A wastepaper basket had been kicked aside. One wall was covered in bookcases that reached to the ceiling and here the intruder had simply gone along each shelf pulling out the books. Some of the book spines were ripped while other books lay flattened as if someone had stamped on them. It was destruction for no other reason that a perverse pleasure. Cass shook her head, unable to understand why anyone would want to do so.

With a sigh, she began to pick up the books and return them to the bookcases. There was work aplenty in this one room to keep her going all evening. Which meant she wouldn't have to see Finn. Which was fine by her. Let him stew in his weird mood. Cass wasn't going to waste a moment worrying about him.

It was good advice but she couldn't keep to it. As she smoothed out pages and tried to uncrease torn covers, she wondered why Finn had reacted the way he had after their picnic. She played it back, frame by frame, trying to understand where it had all gone wrong. More than that, *why* the day had ended on a low. Was she to blame?

Maybe she was. He'd reacted badly when she admitted she was wrong to give up her studies. She had bared her soul to him for a brief moment and then he had reminded her that he was only her boss for a few weeks. That they wouldn't see each other again after that.

It had cut her to the bone. He was telling her that he didn't care what she did. He had no emotional investment in it.

Cass, on the other hand, had invested far too much of herself, too quickly in him. It felt as if her emotions were entwined in him now like ivy on old stones, never able to be pulled apart.

She thought back to the picnic he'd brought to the Park. It had been thoughtful and he'd obviously taken care over choosing foods that he thought would please her. If he didn't care about her, then why bother?

'You're reading way too much into this,' Cass said out loud, reprimanding her inner self. 'He's a man who loves his food, that's all.'

An image of the small red-checked tablecloth flashed in her mind. It made her want to cry. It was an extra touch to the picnic. An unnecessary, sweet touch. If it was just about food, would he have done that? Didn't it signify that the picnic was special?

Cass lifted the chair and turned it upright. She turned her attention to the desk, gathering Finn's belongings from the floor and trying to place them nicely on the desk top. Still her mind stayed too active, mulling over the day.

When she started taking photographs he had been fine. But then, that was his zone. His passion for photography overrode everything. So that didn't count, she argued. But there had been real tenderness when he reached for her. He had touched her skin. She had felt the roughened whorls of his fingertips on the sensitive top of her arm. Not only that, she didn't mind. If anyone else had attempted to touch her scars, she'd have run a long mile. But Finn. She shivered, imagining his touch on her body. Anywhere.

Just as she imagined they were getting close, his expression had clouded and he'd withdrawn from her. She had no idea why. Had he felt a sudden revulsion after all? She'd jumped away, taking the camera and hiding behind it rather than see his face. Realised then why Finn liked photography so much. It was a mask.

She had hidden behind the rocks to compose herself. Waited until she could emerge with a smile. Except that when she'd done that, it had achieved nothing. Finn's face was stormy and his voice clipped when she suggested staying a little longer. She hadn't wanted the day to end on a bad note. If they had lingered, maybe he'd have softened his mood. Just maybe she might have got why he was being so awful.

Instead, here she was, on her knees in his private study, picking up torn pages and scattered paper clips. Her anger had cooled and she felt, all of a sudden, weary from the day.

Cass sat in the deep chair. It was matching maple wood with a wide, curved back that was oh so comfortable. She raised up her bare feet and rested them on the desk, defiantly. Then she tipped her head back and closed her eyes. Just for a few minutes.

★ ★ ★

She was dreaming. Her recurrent nightmare. She was running along a long, endless corridor but her legs moved slowly as if she waded through treacle. Her arms flailed out in front of her and she was drenched in dread as she tried to reach out, to find them. The smell of smoke filled her nostrils.

The floor under her bare feet turned to charcoal and crumbled away. Her soles blistered on the red-hot tiles and a timber, jewelled with glowing flames, fell as if in slow motion, onto her. She screamed their names, scrabbling desperately to get free as the burning wood branded her arms and the stench surrounded her as she rolled and rolled.

Cass woke with a harsh gasp. Beads of sweat dotted her brow. She wiped them away and then gave a cry. She could smell smoke. For real. She half-fell from the chair as she tried to get up and out of the room. She ran into the living room and felt real fear. Grey billowing clouds tongued in through the door from the hallway.

*Finn*. She had to find him. She had to alert him. Get them both out. He was ... he was upstairs ... at his computer. Why hadn't the fire alarms gone off? Cass looked up, scanning the ceiling. There was no alarm box. No telltale white line of cable along the corners of walls. He didn't know the house was on fire.

The smoke was coming from the kitchen. She knew she would have to go past it and up the stairs to get to him. But would she make it in time? Would they both get trapped upstairs? She forced one foot in front of the other until she reached the hall. Her pulse was pounding in her temple and her throat was dry.

'Finn!' she croaked. She shouted again, managing it louder and clearer.

Finn appeared through the kitchen door with a dish towel. He didn't look scared or tense or concerned. He looked embarrassed.

'Sorry. I put bread in the oven to heat it up and then I forgot all about it. Cass?'

Now there was concern spreading over his face.

She was shuddering uncontrollably.

'I thought . . . you . . . I . . . that it was a fire,' she managed, her voice faint.

'Oh, Cass, I'm so sorry.' Then his arms were around her and his big body was sheltering her, easing the spasms of her muscles as she collapsed in relief against him.

She felt the steady pound of his heart as her head lay on his chest. His grasp around her tightened and he held her fiercely, murmuring words that she couldn't catch but didn't need to. She thought she was okay until a sickening rush of tears spilled out of her like a volcano erupting. She cried noisily and messily and he let her. He didn't tell her to stop. He didn't comfort her with more words. He simply held her as the torrent rushed forth.

When there were no more tears and she felt hollowed and nauseous with the convulsions, Finn pulled her with him into the living room and onto the sofa. She sat on his knee, curled in to him like a limpet. He kissed her forehead softly and waited.

'I was dreaming about the fire,' she said. 'It was so real. I was back in my parents' house and I could smell the smoke. I was running, trying to get to them, when the house collapsed.'

'It's okay, it wasn't real. Try to forget.'

'No, don't you see?' She twisted in his embrace so she could look at him. 'I remembered. Usually the nightmare is patchy, no real details, more like impressions of fear and panic and loss. But this was real, in a way. It means something.'

'That's good,' Finn said cautiously.

She shook her head at him, trying to make him understand.

'It's the first time I've cried, Finn. The first time I've really felt it.' She laughed shakily. 'I must look awful. I feel jelly-eyed and blotchy.'

Finn leaned down and kissed her lips. It was chaste and momentary. It was comfort not passion.

'You look lovely to me,' he said huskily. 'I think you're the bravest woman I've ever met, Cass Bryson.'

'Not fragile? Not someone who's about to crumble? In fact, I just did crumble,' she joked weakly.

'That wasn't you crumbling. I think that was you beginning to come to terms with the accident,' Finn said, 'don't you?'

She did too. She didn't question the timing. She knew why it was happening. It was all because of Finn. Her increasing feelings for him were loosening all her clammed-up fears. Freeing her. She wasn't going to try to explain that to him. It sounded like mumbo-jumbo and she could imagine him being mightily puzzled if she voiced it.

'I should get you sweet tea. Isn't that what they give for shock?'

He made to rise but Cass didn't budge.

'Don't go,' she whispered. 'Don't leave me.'

She reached up and kissed him. It started as comfort but slid rapidly into more. Her mouth opened under his and she sought him first. Finn returned it hungrily, kindling her desire with his tongue running on the edge of her teeth and twining with her tongue. Cass put her fingers into his thick hair and steadied her face to his.

Finn stopped. Pulled his head back. Stared searchingly at her with his ocean-blue eyes.

'Are you sure about this?'

Yes, she was sure. Without him, she was drowning. She needed this. *Needed him*.

'Make love to me, Finn,' she said.

Her voice was soft but steady and she locked her gaze with his, letting him know she was serious. She saw his pupils darken and then his mouth was on hers and this time there was no comfort, no hesitation, just pure raw desire.

His touch was gentle but sure as he cradled her head and she felt the warmth of his finger tips on her neck. Her pulse was running wild as he trailed kisses from the hollow of her collarbone along to her shoulders then unbuttoned her blouse. She was lost in the molten surge as her body reacted in sheer pleasure and felt his harden in answer.

She almost didn't realise until it was too late and she had given herself up to him entirely. His kisses, butterfly light on her arms. On her scarred skin. Murmuring her name as he followed the lines and curls that marked her.

Caught up as she was in the wonder of sensations, she didn't pull back. She followed her impulse to stroke across his broad chest, feeling the hard muscles under her fingers as she let them move lower. Finn groaned and the sound excited her. He was big and strong yet she had the power to make him helpless with her body.

The arm of the sofa dug uncomfortably into her back. Finn pulled back reluctantly.

'This isn't designed for what I have in mind,' he said, his voice gravelly.

Cass nodded. 'Agreed. Want to show me your bedroom?'

'Love to.'

Padding upstairs after him had broken the spell. Cass still wanted him but should she do this? She was suddenly uncertain and anxious. What if he didn't like what he saw? She wished she had more experience than just Tom. Wished she could see into Finn's head. What was he thinking? Did he feel sorry for her? Was that why he was doing this?

'Cass?' Finn said, from the edge of his large, king-size bed.

'Don't ask me again if I'm sure,' she said, and her voice trembled, annoying her. 'I'm not but I want this anyway.'

'We don't have to do this,' Finn replied. 'I don't want you to regret it.'

Subtext, he doesn't want to, Cass thought swiftly. She sat beside him on his bed awkwardly. He had seen her scars and now he didn't want her after all. She lay down, her mind empty. Finn lay back too. They were so close she felt the rise and fall of his breathing. She could leave now and it would be alright. He was the sort of man who would be okay with whatever she decided.

Or she could be brave and stay. Allow herself to have this one precious time with him. To remember him by. She wanted him. She needed him. Slowly, Cass turned on her side and reached out. Finn's reaction was immediate. He turned to her and as if they hadn't broken their stride, their lips met and their bodies melded.

There was no need for more words, more discussion. The heat between them rose intensely. Finn's lips were on the curve of her breast, making her skin shiver with delight. His touch left a tingling path of anticipation as they shrugged out of their clothes.

'Yes,' she whispered in answer to his unvoiced question.

Yes, she had no regrets.

'Are you okay?' Finn whispered.

She nodded.

'You don't realise how beautiful you are,' Finn murmured and he pushed her damp hair gently back from her face and kissed her oh, so tenderly.

She was aware of her bareness and tried to pull the cotton sheet over her arms.

Finn wouldn't let her. He deliberately bent his head and kissed each raised welt. She felt the hot pressure of his lips on her and lay immobile. Conflicted. Surely he had to be disgusted by her damaged arms? She squeezed her eyes tightly shut. She couldn't bear it if she glanced up and saw what she had seen in Tom's expression so fleetingly and yet as long as eternity.

He had said she was beautiful and when she was in his arms at the peak of their love-making she had felt it too. Now she was coming back to reality piece by piece. She grabbed at the sheet and covered it over her. Finn let her. Immediately she felt more secure.

'I meant what I said,' Finn said. 'You are beautiful. You don't need to hide from me.'

'I'm not hiding,' she lied. 'It's a little cool, that's all.'

'I could heat you up,' Finn suggested, a wicked light in his eyes.

A heat kindled easily in her midriff. What was it about him? He was addictive and she could never get enough. She was greedy for him. Cass pretended to shiver so that he leaned right in and then she snatched a kiss playfully.

Finn growled and pretended to take the sheet edge. Cass let him. She liked that look on his face when he saw her. She forgot about her arms when his blue gaze darkened as if he'd eat her up. That power she had over him surged delightfully.

They were perfectly matched for this age-old dance of bodies meeting and even if his heart wasn't involved, Cass knew hers was lost forever.

*　*　*

Finn lay drowsy and contented. The sun shining in from the window was still high but had altered from afternoon to evening light. He felt utterly at peace. Happy with the world. An unusual sensation for him. Talking of sensations . . .

He reached over for Cass and felt the empty space. She'd gone. He sat up and rubbed his head. Listened. There was the sound of running water. She was in the shower. Relieved, he lay back, resting on his bent arms. What had he thought? That she'd run away from him?

He hoped she didn't regret what they had done. He didn't. They had no future together. He only hoped she was okay. They both had known the score when they slept together. It wasn't a forever kind of thing.

Now that he'd justified that, why did he still feel a kink of worry about her? He heard the shower turn off and the bathroom door open and shut. The patter of her feet as she headed for her bedroom.

They met up in the kitchen. Finn was fresh from his own shower, his hair still damp. Cass turned as he went in and she smiled. A knot of tension dissipated from his stomach. It was okay.

'Hey, guess what, it's time to eat again. What do you fancy?' Cass said.

'You.'

The word came out without thinking. She looked marvellously fresh and he could smell lemons and lavender from her. Her long, blonde hair was damp and wavy as it hung down her back. Her emerald gaze was clear and steady. He liked her. A lot. If only it was as easy as telling her and letting them see where that went.

But that was unfair to both of them.

He had nothing to offer her. Unless she wanted a period of moving around in places that could quite frankly be terrifying. She was brave but that didn't mean it was right to place her in danger. Finn coped with risk but he only ever had himself to worry about. It would be a different matter having to care for another person too in the situations he often ended up in. Anyway, what was he thinking? Hadn't he decided that a long affair was out of order? And that a short weekend affair was not going to be enough. Which left them where, exactly?

His stomach grumbled and Cass laughed.

'I'd say we eat. What do you recommend off your list?'

'You want to eat out?'

'I was thinking of ordering in, if you don't mind. I've had enough outings for today. What do you say?'

'I say we do whatever you wish,' Finn said, not caring beyond the interesting fact that Cass's hair had bleached in the

New York sunshine to almost pure white.

'Italian? From your favourite place?'

'Mmm.'

'Finn, are you even listening to what I'm saying?'

'Did you know you're the first woman I've had stay over here in my house?' Finn said.

That stopped her in her tracks. Cass laid down the list and looked at him in surprise.

'You must have had a lot of girlfriends,' she said. 'I can't believe you never invited them here.'

Then she blushed. 'Sorry, I didn't mean to imply that you've had hundreds of affairs.'

'Not hundreds,' he agreed, 'but I've had a few. I enjoy dating attractive women but it never lasts long.'

He was warning her. Wanting her to take it on board without him spelling it out. It was for her own good.

'Like Lila,' she interrupted, her gaze abruptly drawn to the marble worktop as if it was fascinating. She rubbed an invisible mark with her thumbnail.

'Yes, like Lila. She didn't want commitment any more than I did.'

'So, it's definitely over between the two of you?'

'Can you even ask me that, given what we've been doing upstairs for the last few hours?' Finn said incredulously.

Cass had the grace to blush once more but her eyes were lidded and he couldn't guess at her thoughts.

'I deserved that,' she said in a low tone. 'It's just that . . . I don't think Lila believes it's over.'

'That's crazy.' Finn let an impatient sigh out. 'She didn't turn up at Biarritz. She hasn't phoned or texted. She sent you in her place. I'll bet she had some other guy in place and that's why she didn't want to waste her Friday travelling over to France. I'm right, aren't I?'

Cass's face gave it away. He wasn't bothered. In fact he was glad. Good luck to Lila and to her new lover.

'Why do you never invite your dates here?' Cass asked.

Nice swerve of subject. Clearly Cass didn't want to talk about her sister either.

'It's easier to go away for the weekend,' he said. 'Neutral territory, no washing up, all meals made for you.'

'That's a cop out. I don't believe you.'

Now her green gaze challenged him.

'You're right. I guess it's really because this is my personal space. It feels too intimate having someone stay.'

'In case they get ideas of it being more permanent than you know it's going to be,' Cass said, a little sharply.

'Cass . . . '

'If you're worried I'm looking for a commitment from you, then don't,' she went on baldly. 'We both know this wasn't meant to happen. We've been avoiding it since we met. But hey, it has happened and it's no big deal.'

'It is a big deal, to me,' Finn said. 'I never wanted to hurt you. I just want us both to know where we stand. I don't do long-term relationships.'

'Finn Mallory, traveller and photographer, footloose and no ties ever,' Cass said sarcastically. 'Heaven forbid he should feel too deeply about anyone in case his perfectly created life falls to pieces. Commander Finn wins again.'

Finn grimaced. She saw right through him. Cass spun on her heel, the restaurant list falling to the floor. She stopped at the door.

'You know, actually I'm not the first woman you've had stay over at your house. I'm only here as your employee so technically . . . it doesn't count.'

\*   \*   \*

Finn laid out his purchases on the worktop. Eggs, salad leaves, fresh pasta, herby tomato sauce from his Italian restaurant, ditto a tiramisu heavy on coffee, cream and liqueur. There was no sound from the rest of the house and he missed it. Cass had gone out for a walk after a vigorous hour of what sounded like drawer slamming and paper tearing from his study. He had kept well clear and finally decided to go shopping for the makings of a meal.

Now he frowned at what he'd bought. It was a long while since he'd cooked. This was for Cass. Somehow he got the impression she liked home-cooked food a lot better than eating out. Something else they didn't have in common. Finn lived on take-out. He never cooked when working on a project. Never did so at home either but he was beginning to regret that, faced as he was now with ingredients but no idea how to put them together.

Her angry words rang in his ear. The last thing he'd wanted to do was upset her. He hadn't meant to make her storm out. But she had to know it was a bad idea for them to start whatever it was. He had his Hidden Places project to finish. After France, there was the possibility of a trip to Russia, across the steppes. Bill Hamilton was investigating it for him and there was the hint of another television tie-in series.

And Cass? Where would she be? Back in London finishing up her language studies? It was for the best. So why did he have a hollowed-out feeling at the idea she wasn't going to be with him? His house, which had always been a sanctuary for him between trips abroad, seemed now empty without the sounds of another human presence.

He was aware he was keeping note of how long she'd been away. His neighbourhood was safe enough, but even so. If she wasn't back by quarter after eight, he was going looking for her whether she liked it or not.

In the meantime, he had to find a method of boiling the pasta. Did the sauce go in the water with it or did it go on after? Finn snapped his fingers. There was an ancient recipe book in the study that had belonged to his mother. Back in the days when she had occasionally played Mommy and cooked for him and his brothers.

His study was immaculate. Cass had done a great job of fixing it back up. All his books were once again in the bookcases and his desk was neatly laid with paper, office equipment and a clean blotter. It came off his mental check list. Basically they were done here. Once he'd finished a few minor changes on his database they could return to France. Or rather, he could. Cass could go home to England. The latest text from Liz's sister suggested she was making such good progress she'd be able to write and take notes.

The recipe book. Focus on that. There it was, tucked away between two journals he was proud of because they had printed his first collection of photographs. He took the old book back to the kitchen and checked in the index for pasta instructions.

*　*　*

There was nothing like a brisk walk for getting rid of annoyance, Cass decided.

A walk round the block here was a major undertaking. At home it would've taken her ten to twenty minutes but where Finn lived the sidewalks stretched wide and long, wound around the heels of the huge skyscrapers. It gave her time out. Which she needed. To get her head round the fact that there was no future for her and Finn.

He hadn't been very subtle about warning her off. The irony of it was she didn't need his warning. She had no intention of sticking around to wait for him to fall in love with her. It would never happen. That was okay because she wasn't in love with him either. She really wasn't. Although she had to admit she liked him far too much. But that was as far as it went.

After Tom, she knew she would never leave herself vulnerable like that again. Okay, Finn had dealt well with her less than perfect body or seemed to have. But that didn't mean he was going to declare that he loved her. No, Finn had made it plain that wasn't his style. He was a love 'em and leave 'em sort of guy.

Fine. She'd be like that too. Never give him an inkling of the emotional affect he was having on her. Keep it purely physical. Her stomach clenched pleasantly as she recalled the early evening's activities. He was a generous lover and tender. She could almost have believed that his heart was involved.

Which only went to show what an idiot she was! Cass walked faster. There were plenty of people about and she wasn't scared. She was too pumped up for that. Then her footsteps faltered. This was probably her one and only walk round the block in New York. The fact was, Finn's house was cleaned up of damage. It had taken fewer hours than originally scheduled. There was no reason for them to stay on.

She turned the corner and saw the lights of his house. It was familiar territory and yet soon she'd be saying goodbye and would never visit it ever again. Her mouth twisted. This was simply a short interlude in her life.

She pushed open the front door and was hit by a wall of rich tomato aroma. She heard water bubbling and male cursing and the clang of a pan lid slamming down fast. She frowned. This was totally unexpected. Then a slow smile spread across her mouth. She tiptoed along the hall and peeked into the kitchen. There was plenty of steam issuing forth and it was kind of hard to see inside. She wafted the steam away. Finn was there, wearing a red-striped chef's apron that looked as if it had come over with the ark. There was a smear of tomato on his cheek and a glimpse of panic on his face. This wasn't Commander Finn. This was Finn Mallory completely out of his comfort zone.

'What are you doing?' she enquired calmly.

'I'm making dinner.'

In a tone that suggested she was the one who was mad. He hadn't looked in a mirror recently.

'Do you want any help?'

'No. No, I'm fine.'

She was actually a little touched that he was cooking for her. It didn't make up for all the problems between them but it was a move in the right direction. She made as if to leave.

'In reality, yes I need help. Lots of help,' Finn said loudly.

Cass sauntered over to the worktop and picked up the piece of paper that lay next to the recipe book. In Finn's neat penmanship was a numbered list of instructions on how to prepare the pasta, dress it with sauce and serve with a side of greens. He had even included when to put out the dessert and switch on the kettle for after dinner coffee. Her mouth twitched. Then she held it in front of him and calmly tore it in two.

'There are no rules when it comes to good cooking,' she said. 'It's all done by instinct and feel and by using your senses.'

There. That felt satisfying. They both knew she wasn't talking about the cooking. Cass's earlier annoyance with him was simmering as much as his tomato sauce, under her calm surface. She had finally worked it out. Why she was so angry. It wasn't that he was not in love with her. She couldn't force him to love her. It was the fact that he hadn't given it, *given them*, a chance.

She was finally ready to do so. He had made love to her as if he meant it. She hadn't sensed any repulsion from him. During her walk she had bravely resolved to allow their affair to develop, if Finn made any move in the right direction. Which right now, seemed unlikely.

'You tore up my list,' he stated, dangerously.

'Yes, I did.' In a 'what are you going to do about it' tone.

'So now if dinner's a disaster, it's all your own fault.'

'That doesn't follow. I'm helping you to get into the creative cooking zone and leave your box thinking behind. You should be thanking me.'

Cass folded her arms and smiled provocatively.

'For tearing up my rule book?' Finn asked.

His eyes glittered and Cass chose to believe it was the steam getting into them. Her heart thumped.

'Yep. For freeing you. So, now you're free what are you going to do?'

'How about this?' Finn pinned her to the wall next the door, moving so fast for a big man that she had no time to react. He leant down and kissed her hard.

'You know what that is?' Cass asked him, her pulse fluttering wild.

'A kiss?'

'No, it's a distraction behaviour because you're not coping with cooking blind. Without your beloved rules. Because let's face it, Finn, without your lists and rules and schedules there's nothing. Nothing that's you. Where's the real Finn when you're not hiding behind the rigid frame you've made of your life?'

The fun had gone, if it had really been there in the first place. Now the words poured out. All her frustration with him and with herself. Her fists thumped on his chest as she spoke, not painfully but enough that he staggered back a step.

Then he hugged her tight and waited it out. Cass slumped in his arms. Pushed him back. Picked up the torn paper and put it back on the work top. Made to go.

\* \* \*

The pasta he'd so carefully weighed and simmered was boiling madly like a geyser. The sauce was blackening in the shallow pan on the other ring. But Finn ignored them. He had a decision to make. And fast. The only woman he had ever had deep feelings for was leaving. She wasn't going far. She was stuck in his house until they flew from the country. But she was leaving him. If he wasn't careful, Finn knew he wasn't going to see the real Cass again. The warm, brave, funny woman he liked.

He had hurt her. His explanation of how he conducted his short relationships had sounded fine to him. But Cass deserved better. He might be proved right in the long term and she might leave him when he never settled in one place for long enough. But didn't she deserve a chance to try? Didn't he? Wow. This was hard. Much harder than walking across a derelict rope bridge over a chasm. Much harder than getting his nose broken in a bar in Hanoi. He didn't know how she felt about him. It didn't matter. All that mattered was that there was time for them to try harder to see what this was.

'Wait.'

She stopped and it seemed to Finn that she looked hopeful.

He took the two pieces of list and tore them further. Twice, then in four, six, eight white patches of confetti. He gave her a half smile. Waiting for her response. Cass stared at him. Then, like a ray of late evening sun, she began to smile.

At that second and with perfect, awful timing, Cass's cell rang. She threw Finn an apologetic moue and pressed to answer. He listened, hoping whoever it was would ring off fast.

'Lila, hey.' Cass pushed her hair behind her ear. 'What's up? Are you okay? You want my address? I gave that to you already. Not that you sent me a postcard.'

There was a pause in which Finn heard the traffic outside, a woman arguing with another, and the blasting horn of a police car racing somewhere to something terrible.

'You're what? You're here in New York?'

Cass looked up at him with an unreadable expression as she spoke to her sister.

# 12

The bar was busy and noisy despite the late hour. New Yorkers never slept, Cass decided. Lila had offered to buy the drinks and was now chatting and laughing with the hunky bartender. Finn had managed to find them an alcove and ordered tapas. The pasta and sauce Finn had attempted had been boiled too long and they had abandoned it. Cass felt a twinge of envy at Lila's breezy manner. Her hips swayed confidently as she walked back across the room towards them, pulling the gaze of every man in the place. She was stunning and she knew it.

'What a friendly bunch,' Lila laughed, clinking the three glasses as she put them down carelessly on the table. 'I could get to like this city so much I might move over here.'

'It's a great place,' Cass agreed, 'but

what would Ant say if you relocated here?'

Lila frowned briefly. 'I'm finished with him. We had a massive blow-up and I threw him out.' Then she brightened and slid a sideways glance at Finn. 'That's when I bought my flight out here. I decided I wasn't going to be sad and miserable. I needed cheering up so here I am.'

'What's happening with Mandy's café?' Cass asked, trying to ignore the sinking feeling in her stomach.

Lila couldn't be more obvious if she tried. She'd dumped Ant and was making it blatantly clear that she was ready to try again with Finn. Cass didn't want to look at him to see his reaction. Despite all the intimacy between them and Finn's firm declaration that it was over between him and Lila, there remained a niggle of uncertainty for her. It didn't help that Lila was practically drooling over him. Did she have to sit quite so close?

'The café's on its way out,' Lila said,

shrugging, 'Mandy's struggling with a mountain of debt and my job was the first casualty. I'm now footloose and fancy free.'

'That's terrible,' Cass said, horrified. 'Poor Mandy. That café was her dream.'

'Yeah well, she should've been a bit more careful about overstretching to take on another café then. She gambled and lost.'

Lila took a forkful of the prawn tapas and popped in her mouth. Her arm brushed Finn's as she did so and Cass noticed he moved his deliberately away. His mouth was set in a polite smile but Cass knew him too well now. He wasn't enjoying this. She felt suddenly guilty. After all it was her sister who had turned up uninvited and forced them all out to socialise.

'So what are you going to do now?' she asked, trying to keep the conversation going.

'I'm going to visit with my little sister, if Finn doesn't mind putting me up?' Lila wrinkled her nose appealingly

241

at Finn and laid two slim fingers on his wrist.

An awful, burning jealousy choked Cass's throat. She pretended to choose from the scattered bowls of tapas, horribly aware of how pale Lila's fingers were contrasted against Finn's tanned arm. Why did Lila have to arrive at this moment in Cass's life?

Back in Finn's kitchen just before her phone rang, she had been sure he was going to say something that would change everything between them. She had riled him up, shaken him mentally by telling him he was wrong to hide behind his work and the way he led his life. At first, she thought she'd gone too far and he was going to be so mad at her. But then, with that single command, *Wait*, it was as if he was going to confess or admit to . . . what? Maybe she was imagining it. The trouble was, now Lila was here literally separating them, Cass knew she had lost the chance to find out.

'No problem,' Finn said, moving his

arm so that Lila had no choice but to remove her touch. 'You're welcome to stay for a few days. After that, I'm afraid Cass and I won't be there.'

'Why not?' Lila flicked a surprised glance at Cass. 'Where are you going?'

'Back to Biarritz,' Finn said firmly. 'We're in the middle of a project over there. We're only here to sort out my house which was ransacked by thieves. Cass must've told you.'

Cass liked that Finn had referred to his project as if it belonged to both of them and she was glad that he wasn't responding to Lila's flirting. He'd told the truth about it being over. Now she just didn't know if it was over between them as well. How could it be over when it hadn't really begun, she wondered. Finn wasn't being completely accurate when he told Lila they were returning to Biarritz. He was but Cass was pretty sure she wasn't going to be.

'I assumed you were working here.' Lila looked accusingly at Cass. 'I thought you were going to be here quite a while. Otherwise I wouldn't have spent my money on coming out here.'

'I'm sure I told you,' Cass said, feeling guilty. 'Besides, I am working here, or rather I was, as the job's done.'

'Great,' Lila said petulantly, 'so I'm going to have to spend even more cash on finding a place to stay if you two are leaving so soon.'

She leapt up and wove her way back to the bar. Cass watched as she leaned provocatively on the bar ledge and whispered in the bartender's ear.

'Sorry,' she said. She looked down at her plate, unable to meet Finn's eyes.

'For what?' His voice was gentle with humour.

Cass looked up then and caught the crinkle of laughter in his gaze.

'You're finding this funny?' she said disbelievingly.

'It's either that or go for annoyance,' Finn told her. 'Come on, Cass, none of it's your fault. You don't have to apologise for Lila.'

'Somebody does,' Cass said. 'She's not making any effort to hide the fact she wants you to let her stay at your house for goodness knows how long. She's dumped poor Ant, probably because he liked her too much and wanted more commitment than she's capable of giving. And she's left Mandy to cope with her problems all alone while she's scarpered over here for a holiday. What kind of person does that make her?'

'That makes her Lila. You're her sister, you must know what she's like. You have to face up to the fact that she's not going to change. So you have to stop taking responsibility for it.'

'Easier said than done,' Cass sighed.

Finn reached for her hand. 'There's something I wanted to say to you.'

Clunk. Three more glasses thrown down on the table. Lila was back, looking prettily flushed. She threw a glance over her shoulder and peeled a laugh at the bartender's wink. Almost immediately she sat right next to Finn, squashing up against him in the small alcove space. Her hair shone in the party lights lit over the windows and her turquoise eyes gleamed with energy and fun. Who could resist her? She was the bright side of the coin to Cass's dark side. If it hadn't been for the fire, Cass thought, mightn't she too look like Lila, bright and bubbly and confident in her attractiveness?

Finn glanced unobtrusively at his watch and Cass wondered what he'd been about to say to her. Would they get a chance to be alone together this evening for her to find out? Or had the moment passed?

Finn excused himself and the two sisters watched him make his way through the crowds to the back of the room.

'He's gorgeous, isn't he?' Lila said slyly. 'How do you rate his kissing?'

'That's not something I want to discuss,' Cass said stiffly, sounding prudish even to herself.

'Oh come on, don't be so stuffy,' Lila snorted. 'You need to lighten up, Cass. That's your problem.'

'And your problem is that you don't know when to give up,' Cass snapped back at her. 'He's not interested in you so stop embarrassing yourself and me by flirting with him.'

Lila stared at her and a slow smile curved her lips. It wasn't a pleasant smile.

'I see. It's like that, is it? You've fallen for him. A word of advice, Finn Mallory doesn't do love and marriage. You're not his sort. I am.'

'Oh Lila, please let's not fight,' Cass said. 'Finn isn't going to take you back and you're absolutely right that I'm not the sort of woman he wants. Can't we just enjoy spending this evening together? We don't see enough of each other as it is.'

'I'm glad you agree with me that you and Finn are unsuited,' Lila said smugly, 'but I'll prove you wrong on whether he'll take me back or not.'

'You're wasting your time. He's not interested.'

'Just because you're still miserable that Tom left you, doesn't mean the rest of us can't have fun,' Lila said sharply.

'Tom didn't leave me.' Cass shook her head, shocked. 'It was a mutual agreement.'

'Mutual agreement,' Lila mimicked. 'You should listen to yourself, you sound like it was a business agreement gone sour. Did you even love him?'

Cass sat back as if Lila had slapped her. She had loved Tom. Of course she had. So why then, had it been so easy to let him go? To tell him to leave her after she witnessed his reaction to her healing body. It should have hurt more to lose him. She hadn't loved him enough. If she compared it to the way she felt about Finn, then she hadn't really been in love with Tom at all.

Which is when it hit Cass with the force of a tornado. She was in love with Finn. There it was. She couldn't help it. But was she ready for it? She had been fighting so hard against her feelings for him that she hadn't realised what they were. No wonder she'd agonised over whether he was in love with her. That was why it mattered so much. Because she loved him. A physical affair was never going be the answer. It would never be enough for her.

'Do you want to know the reason we don't see much of each other?' Lila said suddenly, breaking into Cass's musing. 'It's because you make me feel guilty.'

'What?' Cass was stunned.

'You make me feel guilty for surviving the fire. You act as if every day we should be paying a penance for living while Mum and Dad are dead.'

'While you act as if it never happened,' Cass said, hurt by Lila's words. 'No-one would guess from your behaviour that there was a tragedy in your past.'

'That's sort of the point.' Lila's voice bit with sarcasm as if Cass was daft and couldn't understand the simplest things.

'The point being?'

'The point being that life's too short. We've seen that. Mum and Dad should've had years ahead of them and instead they died in a stupid house fire. I'm not going to waste a moment of my life, even if you insist of wasting yours.'

There was a glint of tears in Lila's eyes and she rubbed them away fiercely. Cass's heart softened and she reached out but Lila swiped her hand away rudely.

'I'm fine. I'm happy with what I'm doing. I'll party and shop gladly until I'm old and I'll enjoy myself to the full. But what about you? Are you going to keep with the hair shirt or are you going to let it go? It wasn't your fault, you didn't set the fire.'

Lila spoke fast and fiercely and Cass felt that for the first moment since her sister had arrived, they were genuinely connecting. Perhaps for the first time in five years.

'I am letting go,' she said quietly. 'I've decided to go back to college and finish my language studies when I leave here.'

'What about Finn? I thought you were going back to France to work for him?'

Cass shook her head. 'No, I'm not. Finn is going back to Biarritz. But I'm going home.'

As she said it, Cass realised it was true. Whatever it was that Finn wanted to say to her, it wouldn't change her mind. She was going to go back to London and start living life properly. In a fantasy world, she would have Finn come and visit her and they would continue their love-making and enjoyment in each other's company wherever that might lead. But in the real, practical world that wasn't going to happen. Finn had projects to deliver and places to go across the globe. He didn't need to be hindered by Cass.

\* \* \*

Finn took his time returning to the alcove. He guessed that Cass and Lila

251

needed space to talk and he'd decided to give that to them by propping up the back bar for a while. For Cass's sake he was willing to put up with Lila. How he'd ever spent a weekend in Paris with her, he had no idea. She was shallow and vain and brittle and there was no substance to her at all. So unlike Cass. *Cass*. Even the sound of her name warmed him.

He had to be patient. When what he wanted to do was run to her and tell her that he had made up his mind to try. He might not be ready to blurt out that he had feelings for her but he was ready to ask her if they could keep seeing each other. Whew. There it was. What was easy and casual for another man was difficult, almost insurmountably so, for him.

Cass had broken through his armour. What had she called it? His rigid frame of life. His protection from emotional harm. She'd boxed it right away with her kisses and sweetly passionate love-making and just by being her.

All his control, built up over many years, was melting away. He had vowed that he'd never let anyone get close to him after suffering from loving his mother and the damage that had come from that. Margaret Conway had been a scarred individual who had taken her sons down with her into a dark place. It had taken all his strength to climb back up and take his younger brothers with him. To survive the final abandonment by their mother. She had chosen to die rather than fight for her children. His answer was to block out the world by keeping a tight control on his life and locking his heart and emotions away.

If Cass was able to deal with her problems and fears, then Finn could do it too. With her at his side. He had no idea how that was going to work when he was going to be in France and then possibly Russia soon after. Still, there were aeroplanes and trains and internet connections. It wasn't impossible to carry on a long-distance love affair.

Besides, he had another idea.

He grinned. His schedule was all over the place, had been since Cass arrived in his life, and what was more he was okay with it. Under normal circumstances, Liz would have been on hand telling him where he was meant to be and when and why. As it was, he knew he had to go back to France but hadn't thought about booking flights or when exactly he should go. *They* should go, he corrected himself. Because he had no intention of leaving Cass behind. That was what he wanted to talk to her about.

He was proud of her for deciding to go back to her studies but selfishly, he didn't want to lose her. He'd come up with a solution. There were internet study courses. That way, she could be with him on his French project and still get back to learning her languages. What better place to do so than in France where she could practise her French all day long. He was impatient to run the idea by her.

Cass and Lila's heads were together as he got back to the alcove and he was struck by how alike they were physically. They were both beautiful women with unusual striking looks but to Finn's mind there was no real comparison. Cass's inner strength shone out when she glanced up and saw him there, rewarding him with the loveliest of warm smiles. It made his heart sing.

'There you are,' she said. 'I was suggesting to Lila that we call it a night. What do you say?'

It was fine by him. It meant he might get an opportunity to talk to Cass at his home about his idea. Lila, on the other hand, didn't seem too happy.

'Cass might need her beauty sleep but I don't. Why don't we stay on, Finn? The night is still young.'

There was hope and light flirtation in her voice, an invitation or possibly a mild challenge. He wasn't going to rise to her bait though. It was enough that Cass's face had dropped in dismay.

'I've had enough for this evening,' he

said easily. 'How about we all go back now.'

'Well, Carlo has offered to buy me a drink so I'll make my own way back,' Lila replied.

'No,' Cass said, 'you're not doing this, Lila, and we're not leaving you on your own in a bar in New York when you don't know anyone. Believe me, you really don't. You have no idea who Carlo is.'

'He's the bartender.'

'Forget it. Get your jacket,' Cass said sternly.

Lila didn't force the issue, Finn noticed and he waited to escort both women to the exit, pleased that Cass had commonsense and was able to instil it into Lila when required. There was steel to her under her fragile exterior. But he was aware of that since he had got to know her better.

'You're no fun,' Lila grumbled, but she put on her light cotton jacket and with a triumphant glare at Cass, linked her arm into Finn's.

He couldn't very well pull away without making too big a scene about it, especially as Lila was pretending it was all a bit of friendly fun, but he wished that it was Cass snuggling into him. Instead, she walked next to him on the other side and he had to be content with the sense of her warm body and the scent of her perfume.

'I'm not staying here.' Lila plumped down heavily on Cass's bed and pouted.

Cass sighed. 'Well you can hardly go elsewhere at this hour of the evening so you'll just have to put up with sharing with me.'

'I didn't mean this bedroom. It's roomy enough to share for one night. I meant New York.'

'Honestly Lila. Back in the bar you were talking about moving over here to live and now you can't wait to leave.' Cass shook her head in exasperation as she moved about, trying to find a place for Lila's enormous suitcase and smaller bags. It was as if she was visiting for months rather than days. 'What is all this stuff? You can't possibly need this number of dresses.'

'I couldn't choose what to wear so I stuffed it all in,' Lila said vaguely. 'Anyway, you're not listening to me. I've decided I'm not going to stay here with you and Finn.'

Cass stopped in the process of folding up Lila's cotton tops. 'Where will you go? I don't get it. You wanted to come and visit me and now you're talking about leaving already.'

'Yeah, well, it wasn't really you I was coming to visit,' Lila muttered.

'Ouch. That hurt.'

Lila had the grace to look briefly embarrassed before she turned a perky shoulder and shrugged it at Cass.

'Let's be honest, I wanted to get back with Finn. He and I had a lot of fun in Paris,' she said with a wistfulness that made Cass want to shake her until her teeth rattled.

'You broke poor Ant's heart and then decided you'd simply walk back into

Finn's life,' Cass said. 'How convenient for you.'

Lila wriggled uncomfortably on her perch on the edge of the bed.

'It sounds a little clinical when you put it like that but yeah, that's mainly what happened. Although I don't think Ant's heart was broken. He was getting a big clingy so I dumped him.'

Cass rolled her eyes. Sometimes Lila could be incredibly dumb. Either that, or she worked hard at not understanding her lovers so that she could walk away unscathed.

'Thing is,' Lila went on, 'I'm too late.'

'Too late for what?' Cass asked with a yawn.

She was tired. Lila wasn't making any sense so she ought to suggest they continue their chat in the morning.

'Too late because Finn is in love with you.'

There was a long silence while Cass stared at her sister, who stared right back at her.

'That's ridiculous,' she said eventually.

Lila shook her head. 'No, it's not. Believe me I'd rather not see it but it's true. Anybody can see he's smitten. I have no idea why.'

Her puzzlement made Cass want to laugh out loud. It was uncomplimentary and yet Lila's genuine bewilderment was amusing. She was mistaken. Finn wasn't in love with Cass. She turned to argue the point but Lila had stretched out, fully clothed on the bed and had fallen asleep with her mouth slackly open.

★ ★ ★

Cass tiptoed downstairs to find some more bedding. Finn had produced a camping bed for Lila which was lying ready beside the bed upstairs. They hadn't got as far as unrolling the accompanying mattress or covering it with sheets and duvet.

She got a shock to see Finn in the living room, sitting in the dark. He had

260

gone upstairs when she and Lila did and she hadn't heard him go back down.

'Cass?' Finn rose up out of the shadows, crinkling his gaze to see her.

'It's me. Can't you sleep?'

He gestured to the mug. 'Couldn't settle so I made coffee. Do you want some?'

It was the last thing she needed. If she drank a mug of it now, she'd never sleep. But she nodded anyway and followed him into the kitchen.

'Lila okay?'

'Yes, she's fast asleep. She's talking about moving on tomorrow,' Cass said hesitantly.

Lila's words were ringing in her ears. *Finn is in love with you.* It was hard to look at him. She wasn't sure whether she was scared to see that he did love her or that Lila was wrong. So she concentrated on the pottery mug with the blue flowers that he handed her. When she did risk a glance, Finn looked tired.

'Going travelling you mean?' Finn asked, referring to Cass's comment. He took a sip of coffee and Cass did too. She didn't taste it but it was hot and caffeinated which was enough for now.

'I think so. She didn't give me any details of her plans but I don't think you need to worry about leaving for France. She'll be gone before then.'

He let a pause lie there while he worked the coffee mug. Cass drank too much of hers and almost choked on it. Her throat seemed tight and closed over. The easiness between them was strangely missing. It was Lila's words. She couldn't forget them.

'Talking of France,' Finn said, and his voice sounded strange, 'I wanted to speak to you about that earlier but I didn't get a chance.'

Cass put down the mug. Waited. Finn fumbled as he set his mug down and it fell to the ground. They both went to pick it up and their hands met and their faces were so close to each other that Cass wanted to kiss him. But she didn't. There was an odd tension to him.

'France?' she prompted.

'I want you to come back with me.'

'What about Liz? I know she's still laid up but she must be nearly recovered by now. I had planned to go home, to London. Remember I said I was going to enrol in my study course again? If they'll let me, I don't actually know if it's possible to slot back in or if I have to reapply totally.'

She was rambling and he was letting her. *Cass shut up.*

'I'm saying that I want you to come back with me whether Liz is better or not. It's not about the job. I'll miss you if you go back to England.' Finn stopped abruptly.

'That's it? You'll miss me.' Cass let the words out plain and stark. 'You want me to give up my plans for the future on that basis?'

She was hurt and angry now. That was it? He'd *miss* her. No declaration of love from him. What was he offering her? A scanty affair while he made his Hidden Places photographs in France and then what? They would go their separate ways.

'No thank you. I've made up my mind to go to London and get on with my life. You don't need me, Finn. I'll only be in the way. Even if you miss me when you get there, it will pass,' she said brutally.

In the still air, the ping of a cell messaging rang loud. Finn took out his cell and frowned. He looked at Cass.

'It's from Liz. She wants her job back.'

# 13

What exactly did Finn want from her?
A temporary affair when it suited him?
He had been honest about how he lived
his life. He dated women but never let
it get too involved. From the sounds of
it, a weekend was as long as he was able
to commit to anyone! If Cass agreed to
go with him to France, how long would
they be together? How long before he
cast her away? Cass knew she couldn't
put herself through that pain.

'Why will you miss me?' she goaded
him.

Finn looked uncomfortable. Was he
going to answer or not? Then he spoke
as if the words were unfamiliar, as if
they were being dragged from him.

'Because we . . . we get along well.
We like each other's company and we
make each other laugh. You're a
beautiful woman and I don't need to

spell it out how much I want you. And you're attracted to me too whether you want to deny it or not.'

Now the dark blue eyes sought hers and Cass blushed at the memories of how he had explored her body so thoroughly, giving her pleasure like she'd never experienced before. She couldn't deny the mutual attraction. But was it enough for her to move country?

'And?' she asked.

Could he say it? Did he love her, like Lila said?

Finn raised a brow. 'Isn't that enough? Many couples manage on less. Come with me to France, Cass, and we'll find out what this is.'

She couldn't tell him she was in love with him. Not when he was so *casual* about them. She wasn't going to bare her soul and then find out that all he was offering was his usual short-term relationship. Why should she be any different from the other women he had dated? There was nothing special about her.

'What would I do in France? Liz wants her job back so I'm no longer your temp personal assistant. So what would I be?'

'You'd be my partner, lover, companion, whatever you want to call it. It doesn't matter, does it? We'd be together.'

Finn's voice was deep and impassioned and at the word 'lover' Cass's heart raced and a thrill ran along her spine. It would be so easy to say yes. To accept the limited offer. To give herself up to the headiness of sheer passion with this man. But Cass knew she wouldn't. It went against all her instincts for survival. All her need for safety, for a risk-free life.

'For how long?'

Finn looked puzzled.

'How long would we be together in France?' Cass persisted.

'The Hidden Places will take me a couple of weeks to wrap up. By then, Bill ought to have finalised the Russian programme.'

'Russia? You'd want me to come to Russia with you?' Cass asked, her temper flaring at his assumption. 'You're asking me to give up on my studies to simply follow you about until you tire of me. No thanks.'

'That's just it,' Finn said with a sudden injection of energy.

He stalked about the kitchen, picking up the salt cellar and putting it down, moving a plate to one side and folding a cloth until Cass was ready to scream but he kept talking and she had to listen.

'That's what I wanted to talk to you about. There's a way you could study and travel with me too. Instead of enrolling in a college course in London, you could enrol online with a college. Think how good your French and Russian will be when you're living in the countries, speaking with the natives. Surely that's gotta be better than reading text books?'

Interesting that he hadn't chosen to reply on the bit where she accused him of eventually tiring of her. Possibly sooner rather than later, given his track record where women were concerned. However tempting his ideas on her future career were, they didn't make up for the part where he'd give her up in time.

Cass shook her head.

'Sorry, Finn. You haven't convinced me it's worth the risk.' To me, she added silently.

Her heart was going to be broken enough when she left. She'd be a fool to prolong the agony by trailing him to France for a few extra days or weeks.

Finn came close. She felt the vibration of air particles between their bodies. The magnetic reaction they never failed to ignite. He towered over her in height and she had to crane her neck back to meet his gaze. When she did so, the tiny hairs prickled on the back of her neck.

'Let me convince you,' he whispered and bent his mouth to hers.

Cass couldn't help it. She responded

like a woman drowning, parting her lips and letting him seek her hotly and urgently. Moulded her body to his, feeling his arousal and triggering her own. She could never get enough of him. He groaned, shifted his weight to match her hips and kissed her long and powerfully.

It took all her will power to push him away. They were both breathing heavily and Cass's lips were bee stung from his kisses. Even while her mind knew it was for the best, her treacherous body was wanting more. Wanting to be inside his embrace. Wanting to lead him to bed where they could make love all night, deeply and properly.

'Okay, you've convinced me we're a great physical match,' she said, and wished her voice didn't tremble. 'But it's not enough. Going to France with you is . . . too uncertain, too risky. Remember, Finn, I'm the girl that doesn't do risk.'

An attempt at weak humour. To deflect from the raw pain of losing him.

Because that was what was happening here. Cass was pushing him both bodily and mentally apart from her. She had to. Without love, there was no future for them. And she wouldn't settle for less.

Finn wanted to bellow his frustration to the world. Instead, he silently clenched his fists to his sides until the knuckles cracked. He was losing her. Bit by bit. With every word he uttered. He couldn't get through to her.

She was standing there in his kitchen and her posture reminded him of his first view of her in the ballroom in the Biarritz hotel. Defensive and insecure. She was hugging her arms around her slim body as if she was cold in the muggily warm room.

He should tell her how much he needed her. Just blurt it out. See what occurred. How the atoms in the air would take his words and wing them to her. See her expression change. That was the problem. He didn't know how she felt about him. Apart from their ability to seek and give sensual pleasure. Was her heart involved? He had no idea. Which was why he'd had the great idea of inviting her back to France so they could find out what this was.

'You say you don't do risk,' he said, 'but you travelled to France and you came over here with me. You've got plans for the future which is great. All I'm asking you to do is modify them a little. Come with me.'

He wouldn't ask again. Refused to plead with her. But it took every ounce of his hard won control not to.

Cass shook her head. She looked miserable but stubborn. He wanted to pick her up and kiss sense into her. Make love to her until she realised they had to be together. Instead, he blew it. He just didn't realise that until it was done.

'This isn't about risk,' he said. 'It's about trust. You don't trust me. You think I'm like Tom.'

He heard her sharp intake of breath but he went on.

'You're worried that you'll see in my eyes what you saw in his. That there's an element of pity in what I feel for you.'

She was holding her arms crossed, unconsciously sheltering them with her hands. He reached across and took them. Flicked up the flimsy sleeves and put his touch to the scars. Cass didn't pull away. She seemed frozen to the spot.

'I don't care about the damage to your arms. Not in the way you think. I'm not repulsed or disgusted by them. All I care about is the pain you went through to get them. Let me in, Cass. Let me be close to you. I'm not Tom. Can't you let go of the past?'

He sounded angry and then he suddenly *was* angry and he saw her flinch away from him. He reached out for her, to say sorry but she darted past him and he heard her footsteps fast going up the stairs.

Finn thumped his fist hard on the work top and the plate nearby jumped off and broke into shards on the floor. He left it there. His hand throbbed from hitting it on marble and he revelled in the pain. He deserved it. He had lost her. He just wasn't sure why.

★ ★ ★

Cass slipped off her dress and hesitated. The mattress and bedding for the camp bed were still downstairs. She hadn't got them, being side tracked by Finn instead. Her heart was thumping so loudly the noise filled her ears. In the end, she lay down on the bed next to Lila and stared at the ceiling.

There was no way she'd sleep. Tears sprang up and slid out of the corners of her eyes to leak down her cheeks and onto the pillow. She blinked them away furiously. It was over. Her very brief affair with Finn Mallory had come to an end. It hadn't lasted any longer than his fling with Lila. Her mouth twisted with the irony of it.

She could forgive him asking her to

274

give up her plans for the future. Finn was a man who took risks. Yes, he liked to be in control of those risks but he enjoyed his bridge crossings, his bar brawls and his travelling in out of the way places. He carelessly thought she could risk her future to join him for a while based on nothing more than a simple bodily attraction.

What she couldn't forgive was his reference to Tom. It had hit at her most vulnerable spot. I'm not Tom, he'd shouted. Can't you let go of the past? How could he ask that of her? She was the person he claimed to want because of her past. It had shaped her strongly. He wanted her to forget the fire, to pretend her skin hadn't melted in agony, branding her and making her what she was.

Finn was wrong. He was exactly like Tom. He saw what he wanted to see. He didn't see the whole Cass Bryson at all.

★ ★ ★

'You're very quiet, didn't you sleep well?'

Lila's voice was chirpily loud as she loaded her breakfast plate with toast and jam.

Cass, in contrast, felt weary to the bone. Three cups of strong coffee had failed to bring the world into focus. She sat at the kitchen table with a slice of toast in front of her that she had no appetite to eat. Finn had not yet appeared from upstairs. She was dreading seeing him.

'No, I didn't sleep well,' she said, slightly irritated with Lila's unbeatable breeziness. 'You took up more than your fair share of the bed.'

'Sorry.' Lila munched on her toast, not looking at all apologetic. 'I conked out last night. Must've been the flying and then staying out late at the bar. Anyway, why didn't you sleep on the camp bed if I was taking up so much space?'

Good question. If only she had simply gone and got the bedding last

276

night and not spoken to Finn. If only they could rewind the hours to before the horrible argument.

'Where's your man this morning?' Lila asked when Cass failed to respond.

'He's not my man,' Cass said grumpily. 'For goodness sake, Lila, why don't you shut up sometimes.'

Lila widened her eyes in mock horror. 'Someone got out of bed the wrong side this morning. Want to tell me what's got you so hot and bothered?'

'Not really.' Cass stood up and took her plate over to the sink.

'Had a tiff with lover boy, have we?' Lila asked shrewdly. 'Could've told you that was a bad idea, Finn likes everything his own way. He's a control freak. You won't win an argument with him.'

'We weren't fighting about anything,' Cass lied.

Lila's comments made a kind of sense. Or would have. Except that Finn had changed. She didn't think of him as

Commander Finn any more. He had let his true feelings show recently and had appeared more relaxed, more ready to let things go their own way. Just not where Cass was concerned. She bit her lip.

As if she'd conjured him up, Finn appeared in the doorway. If anything, he looked more weary than she did. When she dared to meet his stare, she was disappointed. He nodded politely at her as if they had never exchanged more than pleasantries and as if they were simply boss and assistant.

'Good morning,' Lila said brightly. 'Coffee? Want me to put some toast on for you?'

'Just coffee, thanks.'

'Okay. Listen, Finn, I wanted to say thank you for putting me up last night. But I'm moving on today, maybe Cass told you. I've decided to go exploring America until my cash runs out. I've got my return flight sorted but apart from that I'm as free as a bird.'

She laughed, sounding so carefree

that Cass really envied her.

'You're welcome to stay here as long as you wish,' Finn offered. 'I can give you a key to the house.'

'Thanks but I won't need it. I'm heading north, I've always fancied seeing Boston and there's an old school friend there who I'm sure will put me up. What about you two? Are you going back to France soon?'

Cass cut in before Finn could answer.

'I'm sure I told you I was going home to London.'

'Did you? Doesn't Finn need you in France?'

She glanced back and forth between Cass and Finn with a sweetly sly smile.

Thank you Lila, Cass thought. That was about as subtle as a speeding train smashing through a barricade. It seemed that now that her sister had decided that Finn was off limits to her, she was going to help Cass to win him over. Sadly, that wasn't going to happen.

'Finn's personal assistant, Liz, is fully recovered from her injury and is ready to go back to work,' Cass explained numbly.

She didn't look at Finn. She didn't have to. She sensed him sitting, hardly moving except to raise his mug to drink.

'Can't you find other work over there?' Lila said. 'Surely you don't have to go straight back to London?'

'I want to.' Cass's voice was too loud. It stopped even Lila in her tracks. She made a face as if to say she thought Cass was nuts. Then Finn cleared his throat and spoke.

'I'm flying back to Biarritz today. There's no hurry for you both to leave here. If you can lock up carefully for me and leave the key with my neighbour on the left, that'll be fine.'

'You're leaving so soon?' Cass said in dismay.

He stared straight at her then with a bleak expression.

'There's no reason to linger here. I'm

packed up and ready to go.'

He left the kitchen. Lila looked at Cass.

'You're seriously just going to let him walk out of your life like that?'

'There's no point discussing it. You wouldn't understand.'

'I understand that Finn loves you. So why are you throwing your chance away? Don't you love him?'

'I do love him,' Cass cried. 'I'm in love with him. But it's complicated. I'm not like you. I can't give up everything on a gamble.'

Lila looked serious for once. It was so unlike her that Cass did a double take.

'If you're not careful, little sister, you're going to lose out on something precious because you won't gamble. Life is risky whether you like it or not. The question is, what are you going to be left with if you don't take that gamble?'

She didn't wait for Cass's answer. Cass was left alone in the kitchen with Lila's words swirling in her head.

* * *

Finn left in the early afternoon. Cass had already had an emotional parting with Lila. Mostly, it was emotional on her side as Lila was impatient to get going on her adventure and had been on the phone to her Boston friend most of the morning arranging where to meet and what they might do when she got there. She had hugged Cass tightly and then rushed into the waiting taxi, waving madly through the window until the yellow car was out of sight.

She turned back inside to find Finn standing there in the hallway. His case was at his feet. Cass's stomach hollowed. So this was it. He was really leaving. She was never going to see him again.

'You're going,' she said, feeling stupid for pointing out the obvious.

Only, what else was she to say? Don't go. Fall in love with me. Stay with me.

'Yes, I have to go now. Liz has sent me my itinerary.'

Finn forced a grin and Cass smiled faintly back. A shared small moment about his need for lists and order. Only it made her unutterably sad. Everything they said was taking them further from a possible future. Finn was going back to his work and his personal assistant who organised his life to within a minute of each day. And Cass? Where was she going? Home to her small life.

She reminded herself that it was for the best. The possible future she glimpsed would have been a shortly lived one. Then she'd be in a worse position when Finn left her.

She made a real effort to sound normal.

'I hope your project goes well and that Bill manages to get your Russian trip organised.'

'Thank you.'

'Say hello to Sylvia for me. Tell her I enjoyed my morning on her beach.'

'I will,' Finn nodded.

'I hope Liz is really better. That she hasn't gone back to work too soon.'

Cass stopped. She was running out of things to say. Because what she really wanted to say, she couldn't.

'Take care of yourself, Cass,' Finn said gently.

She felt a sob rising up in her chest. So she was glad when he said no more and a taxi blasted its horn outside. She was glad that he didn't try to touch her. Glad that he didn't look back as the taxi took off. Glad, glad, glad.

Once he was gone, she had the luxury of bawling out loud without fear of anyone hearing her. She let the tears engulf her until she felt sick and when she stared in the bathroom mirror her face was swollen and blotchy as if she had some dread disease. She expected to feel better after that and was surprised when she didn't.

She went round Finn's house, tidying up any trace of herself. It was only fair. Then she went upstairs and packed her bags. Her flight didn't go until the evening so she didn't have to rush. She went slowly like an old woman, folding clothes and tucking toiletries into pockets. The house was silent. Without Finn, it felt unwelcoming.

The packing didn't take long enough. Cass sat downstairs, her bags at the front door, Finn's house key in her hand. She would go soon and give it to his neighbour as promised. She wondered where he was by now. The taxi was fast so she reckoned he'd be on his flight to Europe. He was gone.

In the end, she passed the key to the old man next door early after making sure the house was secure. In turn, she took a yellow cab out to the airport and wasted hours eating food she didn't want and reading magazines she couldn't focus on.

The London flight was called late. Cass followed the rest of the queue as it shuffled along to the boarding gate. Her adventure was over. She was going home.

# 14

London had finally got its summer heatwave. Cass moved along the pavement with everyone else, tired and too hot. There was a blister on her left heel and her calves ached. There were no quick fix jobs to be had apparently. She had gone to all the agencies on her list and attended a couple of interviews but hadn't got the position. Today had been spent cold-calling on shops and businesses she had worked for before. All she'd got was politely shaken heads and offers to keep her name on file.

She reached her flat and went indoors to search for a cold drink. Something had to turn up and soon. She didn't have the luxury of not working. It turned out she was too late to apply for next semester studying. In essence, that meant she had a year to wait until she could apply again for entrance anywhere. So much for changing her future. It would have to wait.

She poured a coke and sipped it, staring out the window at the tiny garden at the back of the building. She wondered what Finn was doing. She couldn't stop thinking about him even though she had told herself not to. She had been back a week and it had been a lonely seven days, devoid of enthusiasm for anything. She couldn't seem to pick up the energy to be interested in eating or working or planning for the next week, month or year.

Lila hadn't phoned. It hurt pathetically that she hadn't thought of Cass at all. She was probably having too much fun to bother keeping in touch. Only when she needed money or a lift from the airport would she text. Cass knew that. She couldn't expect her sister to change her personality just because she was lonely.

Once she had eaten an early supper, Cass felt a little better. She was able to give herself a pep talk. It was along the lines of getting on with things, of forgetting Finn, of planning ahead to what she might do. Unfortunately the act of writing ideas on a piece of paper reminded her of Finn's lists and ability to plan so that she laid her forehead on the paper instead and felt the sensation of the cold surface soothe her.

'It's not the end of the world,' she said out loud. 'Lots of people break up and get over it. What makes you any different?'

The flat was silent. No answers there.

'It wasn't even a break-up,' she went on. 'You can't break up from something that never really started, can you?'

The silence was beginning to really bite now.

'So, get a grip,' she shouted. 'Because if you don't . . . '

She didn't finish her threat. She had no idea what was needed to galvanise her into action. The doorbell rang and she was tempted not to answer it. It rang again, longer and with a sense of persistence. Cass sighed. Whoever it was, wasn't going to go away. Probably a sales person with a low monthly sales record, desperate to keep their job. They were going to be sadly disappointed. Cass wasn't going to buy.

She opened the door. Finn Mallory stood there, his large frame blocking the light. Cass didn't move to invite him in. Didn't move at all.

'I was passing, thought I'd drop by, see how you're doing,' Finn said.

'You were passing?' Cass's voice rose incredulously.

He lowered his gaze. Didn't quite shuffle his feet.

'Okay, I wasn't passing. I'm playing hooky for a couple of days.'

'What does Liz think about that?'

'She's absolutely furious.'

Finn risked a grin at her and Cass felt a smile spread across her own face. He was here. Finn was actually standing on her doorstep. He had come to see her. She didn't know what it meant. It might not mean much or anything at all, but he was here.

'So, can I come in?' he asked, sounding tentative and so unlike his usual confident self, that Cass blinked and nodded.

He made her flat seem tiny as she showed him in to her small living room. His broad shoulders filled the place and she had forgotten how tall he was. It gave her a crick in her neck to look up at him. His chestnut hair was tinged with more copper than she remembered and his tan had darkened. Another week in the strong French sunshine, outdoors all day, she guessed.

'Why are you here?' she asked plainly.

He didn't answer immediately, going instead to her window where she had so recently stood and looking out at the garden and its myriad blossoming plants.

★  ★  ★

Why was he here? It was a good question and one that had rattled in his head like the roll of a drum throughout the day as he had fended off Liz's angry questions, packed a light bag and escaped from Biarritz to fly to London.

He turned from the view of Cass's miniature garden to drink in the sight of her. Dammit, he'd missed her so much it was as if he was getting the flu. He'd been unable to concentrate on his photography and hadn't seen the point of it. That had unsettled him. His enthusiasm for his project was at an all-time low. Which was very unlike him. Let's face it, he'd panicked. Suddenly his life's goals had seemed thin like vapour and he had no fixed point to aim at. Or rather, his fixed point had changed. He needed to find Cass.

Now he was here, he had the luxury of reminding himself of every little detail about her. The way her pale, shining hair slid down over her shoulders like a waterfall. The hint of vulnerability in her pool green eyes. The slimness of her waist. She had lost weight, he realised, and was verging on being too thin.

She was wearing a light denim skirt under a pink tee and with a delighted shock, Finn saw she was no longer hiding her arms from view. When he dared to meet her gaze, he saw a strength mingled with that vulnerability that made him feel sure about her and uncertain about himself all in one. Cass had changed. Maybe she didn't need him now. But he sure as hell, needed her.

*Why are you here?*

'I missed you,' he said honestly.

Cass didn't look pleased. Didn't throw herself into his arms. What had he expected? Instead, she seemed to make up her mind about something. Stared at him hard.

'Put your jacket on. We're going out.'

★　★　★

Cass led the way, not waiting for Finn to catch her up. His long strides soon had him walking easily alongside her in any case. He said he missed her. He

292

was in serious danger of making her angry at him all over again. He just didn't get it, did he. Didn't get that missing her wasn't enough. They had had that conversation and Cass wasn't going to go over old ground again. Instead, she was going somewhere new.

After the shortish journey on the tube, they were standing where Cass needed them to be. On the south bank of the glittering River Thames, opposite the Houses of Parliament. Where the London Eye towered above them, a great white circle with the glass pods hanging like fruit from its spokes.

Her heart thumped. When Finn turned to her with a quizzical raised eyebrow, she swallowed nervously before explaining.

'I've lived in London most of my adult life,' she said, 'and I have never been on the Eye. I'm scared of getting into one of those pods and being lifted right up into the sky.'

'So why are we here?' Finn asked and

she heard the genuine puzzlement in his voice.

'Because tonight we are going up together.' Cass turned to him and met his gaze. 'I'm going to take a risk.'

Cass didn't say another word until they had bought their tickets and had gone into the glass-domed cubicle. She took Finn's hand and his warmth seeped into her cold fingers. He didn't speak either and she was grateful for that. The wait until the Eye began to move was interminable and she could hear her own pulse, fast and jittery in her ear.

The view from the great circle was amazing. The whole of London was spread below them, a mass of patterned brick and sparkling lights like a great and beautiful mosaic. Cass gripped Finn's reassuring hand all the way and felt her heart beat slow to a manageable rate. She was doing it. She was facing her fear and finding it not so bad after all. The heady height of where they were and the hard fact that only the mechanical arm and flimsy glass lay between them and a horrible end. But it was okay. And the reason it was okay was right beside her. With Finn, she could manage anything.

Which was the moment when Cass understood that she could never let him go. It didn't matter about her studies or her pride or waiting for him to love her. None of that mattered.

Finn was kicking himself. He had told the truth. He had missed Cass, unbearably so. But he hadn't told the whole truth. Which was that he was in love with her. He had to wait until they stepped out of the Eye and onto firm ground. Cass's eyes were alight with triumph and he was proud of her for taking her risk. Now it was going to be his turn.

'How did that feel?' he asked, grinning at her transparent happiness.

'Weirdly good,' she confessed with a laugh. 'I'm still surfing the adrenaline rush.'

'You took a risk and survived,' Finn

teased. 'Could you get used to it?'

Cass stared at him so intensely that it twisted his guts.

'I could get used to it,' she said slowly, not taking her gaze from his, 'if there was a reason to do so.'

There was a question there that he had to answer. But it was hard for him, so very hard to open up his heart and soul to whatever chaos was out there ready to buffet him.

'I'm not going to Russia,' he said.

*Great, Finn. Take the roundabout route, why don't ya.*

'Why not? What about Bill's contract he was negotiating for you?'

Surprise in her voice.

Finn shook his head. Dammit, he was sweating. He forced the words out and found himself sending up a silent prayer that she wouldn't knock him right back down.

'Because I'm relocating here to London.'

'For a project? A few weeks maybe?'

Cass didn't sound impressed. Finn

had to up his game and fast. He rubbed his forehead.

'For as long as it takes.'

'What takes?'

'Do you really not know?' Finn said softly.

This was it. It was now or never. And he finally got it. There was no going back. He couldn't live without Cass. There was no meaning to his life without her. He only hoped that she would accept what he had to say. And if she didn't? He took a breath. If she didn't, then Finn Mallory had just taken the greatest risk of his life. He was way out of control now. He was reading from no script and no tablet of electronic lists or plans could save him.

'Finn?' Cass prompted.

'I love you, Cassandra Bryson,' he said. 'I fell in love with you the moment I kissed you at the party in Biarritz. It just took me a little longer to realise it. It's not something I planned to do but I can't avoid it and I can't live without you so here I am, in London, where I'm going to settle down and wait for you until you realise you love me too.'

But he didn't have to wait at all because Cass threw herself into his arms and pulled his head down so that she could reach his mouth to kiss him hard. When they came up for air, Cass was speaking but he could hardly hear her for the beat of his own heart as he caressed the woman he loved so intensely and deeply he knew he was lost in her for life.

'I love you too,' Cass said, snuggling right inside the protection of his strong embrace. 'I fell in love with you bit by bit since I met you but I didn't dare hope that you felt the same way about me.'

'You didn't fall in love with me instantaneously when I kissed you as we met?' Finn said, pretending to be hurt.

'Well, maybe a little,' Cass teased gently. 'Love's a risky business, isn't it. And you know I don't do risk.'

'After climbing up into that spindly wheel and circling around in London's sky, I don't think you can say that any more,' Finn reminded her.

Cass kissed him again, just because she could. It was a thrill to remember that she had the right to demand kisses of him any time she chose. Because he was hers. Which reminded her.

'You need to get Bill Hamilton on the phone,' she said, drawing reluctantly away from him.

'Why's that?'

Finn wasn't paying much attention to what she was saying. He seemed far too interested in her lips and the little dip where her neck met her shoulder where his lips nibbled discreetly. They were, after all, still standing on the banks of the wide river in full view of the thinning crowds. What was more, Cass didn't care one little bit about people seeing them.

'Because you have to tell him that you've changed your mind,' Cass said. 'You have to say to him that you are going to Russia after you've finished up in France. But there's one major change in your travel plans.'

'And what's that?'

'There will be two of us travelling to the steppes. I'm not letting you go and have all the fun by yourself.'

'Are you sure? It won't be like a regular holiday destination with home comforts,' Finn warned, but his eyes were bright with hope and love.

'I know that,' Cass breathed and kissed his mouth, oh so slowly and sweetly until she felt his heart race against hers. 'But I'm pretty certain we'll have a well thought out plan of action to follow if things start getting out of control.'

'I've got a plan right now for the rest of the evening,' Finn murmured against her hair.

'Mmm, I can't wait to see if your plan matches mine,' Cass said and kissed him once more.

We do hope that you have enjoyed reading this large print book.

Did you know that all of our titles are available for purchase?

We publish a wide range of high quality large print books including:
**Romances, Mysteries, Classics**
**General Fiction**
**Non Fiction and Westerns**

Special interest titles available in large print are:
**The Little Oxford Dictionary**
**Music Book, Song Book**
**Hymn Book, Service Book**

Also available from us courtesy of Oxford University Press:
**Young Readers' Dictionary**
**(large print edition)**
**Young Readers' Thesaurus**
**(large print edition)**

For further information or a free brochure, please contact us at:
**Ulverscroft Large Print Books Ltd.,**
**The Green, Bradgate Road, Anstey,**
**Leicester, LE7 7FU, England.**
**Tel:** (00 44) 0116 236 4325
**Fax:** (00 44) 0116 234 0205

## MYSTERY AT CASA LARGO

### Miranda Barnes

When Samantha Davis is made redundant, she turns to her boyfriend Steve for consolation — only to discover he is cheating on her. With both job and relationship having vanished in the space of one day, she feels left on the scrapheap, until her mother suggests she travel to Portugal to work at her friend Georgina's guesthouse. There, she meets Georgina's attractive son, Hugo — and the mysterious, taciturn Simon . . .

# TAKE ME, I'M YOURS

## Gael Morrison

Melissa D'Angelo is tired of being the only twenty-four-year-old virgin in Seattle. Before entering medical school, she needs a lover with no strings attached. Harvard Law School graduate Jake Mallory loves women and they love him. But a pregnancy scare with a woman he barely knew birthed a vow of celibacy and a growing need for love, family and commitment. The moment Jake and Melissa meet at a local club, passion ignites. But Melissa can't allow sex to lead to love — and love and family are all Jake wants . . .

# BABY ON LOAN

## Liz Fielding

Jessie is temporarily caring for her adorable baby nephew when she gets evicted from her apartment! She has no choice but to let Patrick Dalton think she's a single mother, so that he'll let her stay with him. The last thing he wants is Jessie and her baby bringing chaos to his serene home — but in no time his life is filled with laughter and the very beautiful Jessie. Until he discovers that his growing love for his houseguests is based on a lie . . .